RED CITY BLUES

A C.T. FERGUSON CRIME NOVELLA (#3)

TOM FOWLER

Editing by Chase Nottingham.

Cover design by 100Designs

 Created with Vellum

My search for a proper business location continued. A month ago, a man came into my home office with a gun. While the encounter didn't end well for him, the whole thing made me realize running a private investigator service out of my house was a bad idea. My quest so far proved both unspectacular and sporadic. I worked a couple cases since then, which infringed on the time I might have spent hunting for new digs.

This meant potential clients could still come to my front door unannounced. One stared back at me now. She was a black lady, at least sixty years old and made of bones and sharp angles. I don't think it would have taken a stiff wind to knock her over; a strong breeze whistling between houses could probably whisk this woman from her feet. Her round glasses looked too big for her slender face. Her hair, a mix of gray and black, was pulled neatly into a bun. She wore a plain white shirt and khaki capris. "C.T. Ferguson?" she said.

"Yes, ma'am."

"I might need to hire you."

I invited her inside, and we walked down the hall to my office. I owned an end-unit rowhouse in the Federal Hill area of Baltimore. Whoever lived in it before I did built a study on the first floor and an addition to contain the kitchen. It and my dining room were a little pinched for space, but I found the trade-off worth it. My desk hid two computers beneath it and held three monitors atop. A binary clock on the wall showed my geek cred to anyone who walked in. My prospective client appraised it all before she sat in a guest chair.

She accepted a bottle of water from my mini-fridge. Today was a typical Baltimore summer day with the temperature and humidity both in the nineties. After a long swig, she said, "Like I told you, I might need to hire you."

"Tell me what happened," I said.

"My name is Erma Johnson."

"Nice to meet you."

"Have you followed the local news recently?" I shook my head. "My grandson was shot and killed about ten days ago."

"I'm sorry," I said.

She gave a fractional nod before continuing. "Three days later, my daughter was murdered the same way outside the funeral home at his viewing."

I couldn't find any words. The level of depravity involved rendered me speechless. For her part, Erma Johnson got through the retelling so far without even a crack in her voice. Defiance flashed in her eyes. She was grieving, to be sure, but she also looked mad at the wanton killer of her child and grandson. In her place, I would have felt the same.

"It's been a week," she continued. "The police don't have no leads. I talk to them every day. The fellow on the phone is always nice to me, but he never has anything good to tell me."

"And you're tired of them not making progress," I said.

"I am."

"Tell me as much as you can."

"The cops say my grandson was killed in a gang shooting," she said, shaking her head. "That boy wasn't in no gang."

"How do you know?" I said.

"A grandmother knows these things."

"Miss Johnson," I said, "how old was your grandson?"

"Nineteen."

Way too young to die. "When I was around his age, I'm sure I did things my grandmother didn't know about."

"No," she said. "My boy wasn't in no gang." Now her voice cracked. *Good job, C.T.; make an old lady cry.* "He was a smart kid, got good grades. He was in college."

"What was his name?"

"Dante. Dante Johnson."

I opened a new Notepad file and entered his name. "Why do the police think he was a gangbanger?"

"He was found wearing gang colors," she said. "I don't know which. He and his mother lived in a pretty rough area."

"No other evidence?" I said when she fell silent.

"Nothing they'll tell me. I've said to the cops that my grandson was a good boy. They say, 'yes, ma'am,' and that's it. I call the next day, and there's nothing new."

"What about your daughter?"

"Anisha was a sweet girl," she said. Her eyes softened and grew wistful. "That boy was the light of her life. It ripped her up when he got killed." Her eyes welled. I pushed a box of tissues across the desk, and she snagged one. "I'm sorry."

"Don't be," I said. "My sister died when I was sixteen. I think I kept the Kleenex Corporation profitable by myself for at least a couple weeks."

A smile played briefly on her lips before disappearing. "My daughter was great," she said after wiping her eyes. "She'd just turned forty. Got her degree a few years ago."

"Was Dante her only son?"

Her head bobbed. "My oldest grandchild. His viewing was last week. We had two—one in the afternoon and one in the evening. Before the second one, a bunch of us were standing outside and talking. A car pulled up, and someone shot my daughter. Shot her down like a dog." Erma Johnson dabbed at her eyes. "Right in front of everyone."

"I can't imagine what it was like," I managed to say as I added Anisha's name to my document.

"I don't know who does something like this," she said. "It's monstrous. It's evil."

It was both those things, but was it also part of a gang's playbook? I'd never heard of it before. "Have the police been able to tell you anything?"

"No. I don't even know if they're trying anymore."

They were, but I sympathized with her frustration. "I'll see what I can find."

"You have a good relationship with the police?" she asked.

I almost laughed. My cousin Rich was a Baltimore police detective. He and I got along, which is the best way to describe our relationship. I stayed on good terms with a couple other cops. The rest found me annoying. I figured it was because I solved a bunch of cases they couldn't. Rich even got a couple of commendations by riding my coattails straight to the awards stage. "Good enough," I said.

"So you'll help me?" Erma Johnson said.

"I will."

"God bless you, Mister Ferguson."

I was about to tell her I didn't sneeze, but I simply smiled and said, "I'll take all the help I can get."

Many news outlets lamented the gang-related crime in Baltimore. Few of them provided any hard facts. They chronicled the shootings, sure, and wailed and gnashed their teeth at all the right times. Beyond a body count, however, they offered little else. The biggest facts I learned from an hour of research were the names of the two biggest gangs in the city: The West Baltimore Buccaneers and the West Side Pirates. In the business world, two organizations with similar names and purposes were likely to merge. On the streets of my city, they shot at each other and anyone else who happened to get in the way.

As their names suggested, both operated in the western part of the city. Public information didn't tell me much more. I turned to the BPD to fill in the considerable gaps. During my first case, Rich left his computer unguarded for a couple minutes, during which I snagged his IP and physical addresses. Armed with those, I mapped the entirety of the BPD's network and got it to accept my laptop as one of its own computers. This gave me access to their files and resources.

They accumulated a ton of information on gangs. I copied some of the more interesting-looking items to review later. One thing they lacked was any history of what happened to Erma Johnson. Never before in the BPD's files was a young man killed, then his mother shot to death outside the funeral home where he lay. I couldn't fault them for being stumped. Additional research told me an identical crime happened in Oakland, California, eleven years before. Two crimes on opposite coasts more than a decade apart was about as far from a pattern as something could be.

I went back to the local angle. Despite a few smaller street crews battling for chunks of turf, the Bucs and Pirates committed most of the crimes. Erma Johnson gave me her daughter's address. It was smack-dab in the middle of Pirate territory. They wore red. I called up Dante's case file. Photos from the crime scene showed him in a rumpled blue T-shirt and a blue bandanna sitting askew on his head. The Bucs, naturally, wore blue, because gangs aren't original when it comes to color schemes. Erma said he was a smart kid. I believed her. My problem was if he were smart, he would've known better than to wear a shirt and bandanna which may have gotten him shot. If he were a Buc, he wouldn't have been alone. I found no record of anyone else getting shot in the area the same day.

Based on what I'd seen, I believed Erma Johnson: I

thought her grandson was a smart kid who was not in a criminal group. Why, then, did he wear clothes advertising his allegiance in the heart of enemy territory? I doubted I would find answers poring over the BPD's scattered info.

I tried a more direct approach.

* * *

AN HOUR LATER, I met Detective Paul King for a late lunch (or early dinner) at The Abbey, recent winner of an award for serving the best burgers in Maryland. I wouldn't quibble. They also boasted of a great beer selection and a convenient Federal Hill location I could walk to in a few minutes. When I entered, King waved from a table against the left wall.

Some people have a youthful or haggard quality working to subtract or add years to their ages. Not King—he was in his mid-thirties and looked it. A mop of disheveled dirty-blond hair sat atop his head. He was about six feet tall, giving me two inches on him, and we both weighed in somewhere in the one-eighties. Depending on our meal choices, we both could tip the scales at a higher number after this.

"Thanks for coming," I said as I slid the chair out and sat.

"How can I say no to The Abbey?"

"No reasonable man could."

A waiter with a hipster goatee and glasses to match asked if we were ready. We were. King built his own burger; I opted for the spicy and excellent Santa Fe. We each chose bottled beers of potent hoppiness and difficult pronunciation. "What do they call this?" he said when the waiter walked away.

"What do you mean?"

"This meal. You have a late breakfast or early lunch, you call it brunch. Every fucking restaurant in the city goes crazy for brunch on the weekends."

"There's no later-in-the-day equivalent," I said. "You can't call it 'dunch.'"

"Or 'linner,'" King added.

"They're both terrible." The waiter returned long enough to drop off our beers. I sipped mine. "This, however, is not terrible," I said.

A few more tables filled up. The bar could claim a few open seats, but much of the small dining room was occupied, at least on the first floor. I only sat on the ground floor of the original Federal Hill location, and only on the second floor of the newer Fells Point spot. Call me old school, but I preferred the original. Being able to get there and back with a short stroll no doubt helped. "It's damn good," said King. He set the bottle down. "You didn't say much about why you wanted to talk."

"Can't it be to soak up your charming personality?"

"No, it can't."

King's personality wasn't as bad as he let on, but it would not be counted first among his virtues. "Your words, not mine," I said. "I need information on local gangs."

My statement made King laugh. His frivolity was interrupted only by the waiter delivering our food. After we had both sampled a few bites of our burgers and fries, he continued. "What makes you think I'm the man to see?"

"I know you've worked in a lot of different units," I said, "including some time on the gang detail."

"You think the bangers talked to me a lot?" he said. "Look at me. I'm as white as fucking Casper the Ghost. They ain't telling me anything."

"You must've made some contacts," I said. "Informants. Something."

"I knew a few guys I could get a little from."

"You still talk to them?" I said.

"I'm in vice now," said King. "I've been upgraded to a different class of lowlife."

"You must have a name for me." I ate some more of my Santa Fe burger. The fresh jalapeños gave it a wonderful heat. I didn't care for food only hot for the sake of it, but I was a fan of honest spice.

"I can give you one. Not sure you'll like it, though."

"Why wouldn't I like it?" I said.

"The guy's a pimp."

I shrugged. "We all gotta eat."

"You're OK with a pimp?" King shot me a quizzical look.

"Better than a drug dealer," I said.

King frowned. "I guess. I'd rather not have to deal with either one, though."

"I think you're in the wrong business."

"Maybe I'll get to Homicide with your cousin one day," King said.

"What's the name?" I asked, steering the conversation away from King's career ambitions.

"Romeo," he said with a straight face.

When he didn't follow it up with anything, I said, "Seriously?"

"Romeo," King confirmed.

"A bit on the nose, isn't it?"

"Christ, you should hear some of the names these assholes come up with. Pimps and bangers love to think they're creative."

"Where can I find this Romeo?"

"Downtown," King said. "His girls used to work the Block plus a street or two over."

I downed a healthy swig of my beer. When I started doing this job almost a year ago, I figured I would sit at my computer and solve problems via my hacking skills. While I still got to be a keyboard warrior some of the time, I spent more hours than I expected hitting the streets, getting into fights, and dealing with characters like a pimp named Romeo. I didn't know how many more beers it would take to make this seem normal, but the number would leave me staggering back home. "Sounds like a fun way to spend an evening," I said.

"It's the Block," King said. "Everybody has fun."

CHAPTER 2

A few hours later, I went out to dinner with Gloria Reading. She and I enjoyed a relationship of fun and convenience—"friends with benefits" as I might have called it in college—though we'd definitely grown closer over the last couple months. Gloria came from a wealthy family like I did, and she didn't need to work a day in her life. Recently, her socialite tendencies got scaled back, and she took a greater interest in my cases. Including this one.

"Gangs?" she said with a delicate frown.

"I'm not convinced the kid was in one," I said.

We ate at Slainte, an Irish pub in Baltimore. When I first met Gloria almost a year ago, she turned her nose up at any restaurant not proudly displaying its Zagat ratings and Michelin Stars in the front window. As she came around in other areas, her willingness to try other types of places increased. One of these times, I would get her to try bangers and mash, but it wouldn't be tonight.

"But he could have been."

"Maybe," I acknowledged. "It seems unlikely, though." I went over my reasons with her.

"It sounds like people in a gang killed him," said Gloria after ruminating on my logic.

"And his mother. It takes a particular kind of barbarism to shoot a woman in front of a funeral home while her son is lying inside."

"This sounds like another dangerous case." Gloria's brows furrowed in concern.

"I do seem be taking a lot of those, don't I?"

"You do," Gloria said. "It concerns me." She reached across the table and grabbed my hand. Before either of us could realize the awkwardness and pull back, our waitress brought dinner. It gave us a convenient excuse to pull apart. The red-headed server set a loaded plate of bangers and mash in front of me and a burger and fries before Gloria. A few months ago, I couldn't fathom her eating a burger, even if she accidentally wandered into a place serving them. I quite liked this newer version of Gloria. She still cut it in half, however, and rarely ate more than fifty percent. But it was progress.

"Aren't your parents worried, too?" Gloria asked once we had both sampled our entrees.

"They are," I said. "We've had a few conversations about it."

"They haven't threatened to cut you off?"

"Not yet." Almost a year ago, I became a rather reluctant employee of my parents' charitable foundation. I took on clients who needed my services but couldn't pay, and my parents cut me a check once I solved each case. They weren't thrilled with the arrangement. Neither was I at first, but I've come to appreciate the work I do over time. My parents still harbored concerns for my safety. I couldn't blame them—I did, too, sometimes. When I decided to do this job, I figured I could remain aloof and use my considerable computer skills to divine the answers. Reality put me on the streets mixing it up with ne'er-do-wells more often than I liked.

"Do they know you've taken this case?"

I smiled and said, "Not yet" again.

Gloria ate another bite of her hamburger. With the amounts she bit off, we would have time for a long conversation. "Are you going to?"

"I'm sure it'll come up at some point," I said. "For now, I'm more concerned about figuring out how to find whoever killed this kid and his mother."

"Of course," she said. "Do you have any idea how to start?"

I shrugged. "The way I usually work. Look some things up, try to make heads or tails of them, ask people questions, hit them when they get mad about it, and see what happens."

Gloria grinned in spite of herself. "That's not much of plan."

"It's usually all I have this early," I admitted.

"What if turns out a gang did it?"

"Then I'll turn it over to the police. They're better equipped for something on a large scale."

"Good." Gloria's chest went out and in with her sigh of relief.

We finished our meal and passed on dessert. My refrigerator contained an abundance of blueberries, so I baked them into a pie. My oven work can be spotty, but my pie game is strong. As I reached for the check, my phone vibrated in my pocket. Earlier, I set an alert to notify me of suspected gang violence in Baltimore. The notification told me another young man had been killed in a shooting being attributed to one of the nefarious organizations.

"Something important?" Gloria said.

"We might need to take a rain check on dessert," I said.

* * *

I MADE Gloria a small sundae for dessert, then busied myself in the office. Paul King told me he used a contact named Romeo. I searched the Baltimore Police Department's records. It didn't take long to find information on Romeo. The moniker proved popular among pimps, but only one owned a file worth mentioning. He was a known procurer of women who managed to avoid arrest and passed that luck onto his girls. He also spent a violent youth in both prominent Baltimore gangs. In homage to his history, all his girls dressed in red and blue. Romeo suddenly became a very interesting fellow.

"I have to run out," I said as I walked into the living room.

Her feet curled under her on my sofa, Gloria polished off her sundae. "You work the strangest hours."

"And I talk to the strangest people. Tonight, I'm going to chat up a pimp."

Gloria blinked a few times. "A pimp?"

"Not my first choice," I said, "but I think he can help."

"Be careful," Gloria said. She stood and gave me a

lingering kiss before I left. It was the kind of kiss to weaken my knees and make me want to stay. I left while I still could.

I parked my car in a 24-hour garage just off Baltimore Street. The sights, sounds, and smells of The Block hit me before I stepped onto the pockmarked sidewalk. Tacky neon signs advertised nude girls and strip shows with the unwritten promise of more. Music best left on a porn producer's cutting room floor blared every time a door swung open. Even on the street, I smelled booze, cheap cologne and perfume, and cheaper women.

I saw several of said ladies of the evening walking around trying to look less conspicuous. Their short skirts, ridiculous boots, and push-up tops always gave them away. My keen powers of observation served me well as a private eye: Along with everyone else on the street, I could spot the working girls. I didn't see any pimps until I looked closer; they popped in and out of the clubs or emerged from the shadows next to buildings.

In bygone years, the Block was longer. More recently, it traded overall length for an uptick in quality. Larry Flynt's Hustler Club brought a higher-class clientele. Sleazier clubs surrounded it, but not as many as before, and not for as many city blocks. The most interesting fact about The Block is it butts against Police Headquarters at its eastern end. It forced more interesting action farther west.

I noticed a few girls dressed in red and blue but didn't see their pimp. The hookers would talk to people and wander off with johns. I never noticed anyone hassling them. Perhaps Romeo gave his girls a little more leash than the traditional late-night proprietor. Regardless, I didn't see him anywhere, so I did the next best thing: I approached one of his girls.

She was white and looked to be in her mid-twenties but was probably younger due to years added by the street. Her blonde hair was natural if a little flat and stringy. Still, she showed a pretty face with delicate cheekbones and stormy gray eyes. I guessed her at five-seven and about a hundred and ten pounds, making her a little skinny for my tastes. She smiled at me as I walked up to her; I noticed she still had all her teeth. No meth, at least.

"Looking for a good time?" she said.

"Actually, I'd just like to talk," I said.

"You a cop?" The smile disappeared so quickly I wondered if it had ever really been there.

"Do I look like a cop?"

She studied me for a few seconds. "You got a cop's eyes."

"Cop eyes don't have depth and sensitivity like mine." This logic failed to persuade her, so I tried a different tack. "Look, I'm a private investigator working a case. I don't care how you make your money. I only need a bit of information, and you're the best person I can get it from right now."

She studied me again before finally nodding. "All right. The pay is the same, though, whether we talk or fuck."

"Ah, romance," I said.

* * *

WE ENDED up at Crazy John's Restaurant and Arcade. Crazy John's had never been the safest place around, but it gave me a good view of the Block and the people who walked up and down it. Sandy—I don't know if it was her real name, but it didn't sound like a faux glamorous hooker name—ordered a basket of chicken wings and fries. I didn't want to eat anything, but to keep up appearances, I got a slice of cheese pizza. We each drank iced tea with our meals. I nibbled my pizza while Sandy tore into her wings as if they were the first things she'd eaten all day.

The meal set me back about sixteen dollars on top of the two bills I paid Sandy for her time. Thankfully, I could afford to live the kind of thrilling life which led me to eat late meals with prostitutes in restaurants growing less safe as the night wore on. When it looked like Sandy slowed her breakneck pace, I started in with the questions. "I hear you work for a fellow named Romeo."

She nodded and washed down a mouthful of food before answering. "Yeah, for a few months now."

"How's he treat you?"

"Really well. He comes around for his money, of course, but he ain't up in our grills all the time, y'know?"

"From what I can tell, he does seem rather *laissez faire*."

"What the hell does that mean?"

"It doesn't matter," I said. "Tell me about Romeo."

"Why you wanna know?" Her eyes narrowed.

"I don't care how he makes his money, either. I'm working on a case, and I think he might be able to give me some insight into it."

"What kind of case?"

"The kind where three people are dead."

"Jesus," Sandy said, "Romeo ain't no killer."

"He's not a suspect."

"Who is?"

"Right now, nobody. Like I said, I need some insight from your boss."

"Romeo's nice, but there's . . . a dark side to him. Like he's got some stuff in his past, or something."

"Haven't we all?" I said. If only she knew how well-drawn her impression was. "You said he pretty much leaves you alone. Does he ever get violent?"

"Not with any of us," she said.

"What about with the johns?"

"Sometimes they need to know their place."

A few people wandered in and out, but the restaurant never threatened to fill up. No one wanted to remain in Crazy John's for long, me included. "Does he put them in their place," I said, "or does he have someone who handles it for him?"

"He's got a big guy with him most of the time. Calls him Tank."

"Is Tank aptly named?"

Sandy nibbled on fries before answering. She was smart enough to keep her voice as low as she could while we were talking. I tried to find a secluded table, but between the other patrons and the arcade games, there was a decent amount of ambient noise. "He's a big boy," she said. "Probably as tall as Romeo but twice as wide."

Right after Sandy finished talking, I spotted someone outside Club Pussycat across Custom House Avenue from the Hustler Club. The combination of street lights and neon made him easy to recognize. Other than a wispy mustache, he was a dead ringer for Romeo's police file photo. He wore a blue tank top over red leather pants and talked to someone who could have played offensive line for the Ravens. The big guy sported a black T-shirt, a red leather jacket, and blue jeans.

"There they are now," I said.

Sandy ducked. "Oh, God, I hope they don't see me. We ain't supposed to eat with the johns."

"I'm not a john, and I paid you for your time, so his cut is the same." She didn't sit up. I shrugged. "I'm going to go talk to him now. Stay here for a while and avoid him if you think he'll give you any grief."

"All right," she said. "Hey, thanks for dinner." She gave me a sort of uncertain smile, like she sought approval. How had this girl come to be a hooker? She didn't strike me as the sharpest knife in the drawer, but she also wasn't a spoon in a tray of knives. At least Romeo treated her well. I reminded myself I couldn't save everyone, and not everyone wanted to be saved.

"Thanks for the information," I said. I got up from my chair, walked outside, and trotted across the street. Romeo stood in the same spot, but Tank no longer loitered near him. Based on Sandy's description, he should be easy to spot. "You must be Romeo," I said as I approached. Still no sign of Tank.

"Who's asking?" he said. "You a cop?"

"Do I really look like one?"

He stared at me for a few seconds, much like Sandy's appraisal. "A little around the eyes."

I shook my head. "I'm not a cop," I said. "Only a man who needs a little help."

"Shit, man, I got girls for that. Go find one of them."

"I don't need them. I need some insight, and I've heard you're the man who can provide it."

He looked me up and down again. "What if I don't want to give you no insight?"

Before I could answer, I saw something dark speeding toward me. In the fraction of a second before impact, I knew I had no time to mount a defense, so I tried to brace myself as best I could. It felt like a truck hit me across the shoulders, so preparing for impact did nothing. I went airborne and only saved myself from a face-plant by twisting enough to land on my left side. My shoulder and hip slammed into the pavement, taking most of the impact, and I skidded before rolling over a few times. Only a brick wall stopped me when my back smashed into it.

Most of my upper body hurt. The roll into the wall knocked the wind out of me, so I gasped for breath as Romeo and the largest man I'd ever seen approached. Tank. I guessed him to be six-nine and over 350 pounds. The wallop he packed earned him his nickname, but his size belied a surprising amount of stealth and speed; I only saw him coming at the very end. If Tank decided he wanted to stomp on my head until it burst, I doubted I could do much to stop him.

Romeo crouched near me. "A man don't like to be disturbed while he's working," he said quietly.

"Paul King . . . sent me," I managed to say between ragged breaths.

"Shit. *You're* the one he told me about?"

"Not expecting someone so handsome?" Breathing came easier now.

Romeo snorted. "You ain't looking so fine right now."

"This pavement isn't a good color for me." I dragged myself into a seated position. Tank looked down at me, too. He stared ahead, looking menacing—which he was very good at—while Romeo handled the banter.

"King said you needed information."

I nodded and immediately regretted it when my neck throbbed. "Yeah," I said around a wince, "about the gangs in particular."

"All right," Romeo said after a sigh. "Let's the three of us go somewhere and talk."

"You won't need him," I said, jutting my chin toward Tank.

"You think you can stop him from coming with us?"

"Not really," I said.

Tank grinned down at me. It didn't make him any less menacing.

CHAPTER 3

Of course, we went to Crazy John's. I got another iced tea, lamented the lack of Vicodin on the menu, and paid for Romeo and Tank, the latter eating enough for a family of four. Once we were seated and food covered every available inch of the table, I got down to business. "Did you hear about the woman who got shot outside the funeral home?"

"Yeah." Romeo shook his head. "That was fucked up."

"Her son got murdered a few days before. He's suspected of being in a gang. I need insight into them. I heard you spent a few years inside, and they let you walk away. I didn't know they often showed such generosity."

Romeo flashed a brief, rueful smile. "They don't."

"A grandmother came to me after burying her grandson and daughter. I'm trying to help her. You graduated to a more . . . service-oriented industry. I need the knowledge you racked up about your former life."

"Ain't my favorite subject," Romeo said, "but I'll see what I can do."

Across the street, one of Romeo's girls picked up a john. They walked toward the far end of the Block. "Your girls are going to be all alone," I said.

"They be OK," Romeo said.

"You sure you don't want The Mountain here keeping guard over them?"

Romeo smiled. Tank didn't even react, like he hadn't heard me. He studied the other patrons. "My girls look out for each other," Romeo said. "Besides, I make them take a self-defense class when they start."

"Really?"

"Sure. This shit ain't feather boas and Cadillacs. It's a business. Being whores means they gonna get taken advantage of. Me and Tank can't be everywhere. I had to learn to fight when I came up. They should, too." He paused. "So you working the funeral home shooting."

"The grandmother hired me," I said. "She swears her grandson wasn't in a gang."

"What do you think?"

"I don't know yet. All signs at the crime scene indicate he was."

"What do you mean?"

"He was wearing blue in the wrong part of town." I noticed Tank glancing around, rarely letting his eyes sit still on something. He didn't look at me, but I knew he knew I noticed him. I didn't think he missed any details. If indeed the price of freedom is eternal vigilance, Tank paid his share in full.

"Bangers get shot all the time," Romeo said.

"When you were in, you knew whose territory was where, right?"

"Of course."

"If you were to go behind enemy lines by yourself, you wouldn't flaunt your colors, would you?"

"No way, man. That's just asking to get shot."

"You put your finger on my problem with the case," I said. "Dante Johnson was a smart kid."

"Don't mean he was street smart."

"No, but it means he wasn't an idiot. Only an idiot would go alone into the wrong territory in colors."

"You don't think he was a banger, do you?" Tank said.

"I don't know yet," I said. "I think it's possible."

"Maybe," Romeo offered.

"In the meantime, what can you tell me about gangs?"

Romeo and Tank looked at each other and laughed. I frowned, and it amused them. "Did I say something funny?" My question triggered a new round of frivolity.

"Shit, man," Romeo said, "how long you got?"

"As much time as it takes," I said.

"We don't. Me and Tank got a business to run and images to keep up. Talking with a cracker like you don't help either one."

"You silver-tongued devil."

"Why don't you just tell me what kind of insight you want?"

A few more patrons wandered in. Crazy John's wasn't crowded, though, so we maintained our privacy. "Why don't we start with which one you were in."

"Both, sort of," said Romeo. "I tried out for the Bucs. Didn't make it. Then we moved a few blocks away, and I passed my initiation into the Pirates."

"How? Did you have to kill someone?"

"Man, you watch too much TV. You gotta do something, sure, but it's usually just knock over a store or beat up a bum. For me, it was knock around an old biddy always used to yell at us."

This cemented the gangs as bullies for me, and I hated bullies. An unfortunate encounter with one in fifth grade compelled my parents to enroll me in private school and martial arts. In high school, I got in trouble a few times defending other students from the assholes who preyed on them. "Then you were in?" I said.

"No. To celebrate, they brought me back to base and kicked the shit out of me."

I felt myself recoil. "What?"

"Yeah, man. Hollywood don't tell you that. They make it seem like all you gotta do is cap some old man. The reality is you're only in after they finish beating you down." Romeo ate his sandwich as if he engaged in this kind of chit-chat every day. For my part, I felt glad I didn't order any food. This part of the conversation would have made me lose my appetite.

"How far up in the gang would a kid of nineteen be?" I asked.

"Depends on when he started. Could be a new recruit, could be one of the big dogs."

"How high up were you at nineteen?"

Romeo sipped soda while he thought about it. "Third in command," he said. "Ran my own crew. I'd been in the Pirates almost six years by then."

I nodded. "What about retaliations? How fast were they?"

"Someone else dead?" Tank said. He paused eating his regal feast—chicken fried steak, onion rings, an already-consumed order of mozzarella sticks, and gravy fries—long enough to ask a question.

Damn. I hoped to pass my query off as casual curiosity. "Another kid tonight."

"How long since the first one?" Romeo said.

"About a week."

Romeo shook his head. "Awful slow."

"How quickly did you get back at the Bucs in your day?"

"Soon as we could."

"You see why this doesn't add up for me," I said. "It kind of looks like gang violence, so everyone wants to write it as such. I'm not convinced."

He nodded and went back to his sandwich. My feeling was when he finished the sandwich and fries, my time would be up. "The first kid's mom got shot, too?" he said after a moment.

"Yeah. Did you go after family often?"

"No," he said.

"Mothers were off limits," Tank added.

"We might try to recruit your little brother," Romeo offered. "But we wouldn't go shoot your momma."

"How could I find out for sure if these kids were in a gang?"

"Shit. Your best way is to talk to the members."

I smirked. "I'm going to guess they probably don't want to talk to someone like me."

"Ain't no 'probably' about it," Romeo said.

"I'll hope to find another way, then."

Romeo grabbed an unused napkin and wrote on it. "This is my number," he said. "I don't know if you'll need anything else, but if you do, call. We want to help." For his part, Tank offered a fractional bob of his head.

"Thanks." I slipped the napkin into a pocket.

"You know, you ain't bad . . . for a cracker."

"I think I need to update my business cards," I said.

* * *

THE MEDICAL EXAMINER'S office wasn't far, so I stopped there after my chat with Romeo and Tank. The ME shares results and information with the BPD, but they maintain a separate network. I could break into the former if I wanted to, but I always found what I needed via other means. One was waiting for the BPD case file to be updated.

This was the more direct approach.

A few months ago, I discovered a doctor at the ME's office released the body of a murder victim to her killer. In return for not broadcasting the fact, Dr. Gary Hunt agreed to supply me with information when I needed it. He usually worked nights, including this one.

"Oh, Christ," he said when he saw me walk in. "What now?"

"You're awfully salty for a man who didn't get fired and led away in handcuffs," I pointed out.

"Can't I just be unhappy to see you?"

"I don't care as long as you tell me what I need to know."

Dr. Hunt sighed and ran a latex-gloved hand through his thinning brown hair. He stood an inch or two shorter than me and possessed a classic runner's physique. I doubted he would ever invite me to join him in a constitutional, however. "Fine. Give me a few minutes. You can sit anywhere."

I grabbed a chair in the waiting area. It was like the ones in hospitals, only shrunk in square footage by a factor of ten. My seat looked the most comfortable of the six. A solitary and shabby table held the last three issues of *The Baltimore Sun*. I found it an odd choice. Family members waiting to identify a body shared the space with articles about their dead relative. Even the shitty magazine selection at every doctor's office would have been better.

After about ten minutes, I almost got desperate enough to pick up a paper and read it. Dr. Hunt spared me my moment of weakness by returning. "Wanna come to my office?"

"You don't have another body to process?" I said.

He shrugged. "They're dead. The wait won't kill them. Come on."

We walked down the hall and into a small room. If a messy desk were a sign of genius, Dr. Hunt was a savant. Papers, file folders, plastic cups, food wrappers, and assorted other detritus consumed almost the entire surface. His keyboard—its cleanliness was a mystery I would never solve—sat as an oasis amid a desert of disinterest. Any photos a normal person would have on a desk were bumped to the bookshelves. I saw pictures of the doctor and his wife interspersed among books whose organization impressed me. The office made less sense the more I saw.

"What's up?" said Dr. Hunt, snapping me back into the moment.

"A kid killed tonight," I said, calling up the alert on

my phone. "Andre Carter."

"Sad. He was young."

"I was hoping to learn more from you than I did from fifteen seconds of Google."

"I don't know a lot yet. He's pretty fresh."

"Let's do some comparisons, then," I said, hoping to draw Hunt out of his reticent shell. "I'm also investigating the deaths of Dante and Anisha Johnson."

Hunt frowned as he started typing. "Those names are familiar."

"Dante was shot. Police are calling it a gang shooting. A few days later, his mother met the same fate outside Dante's funeral home."

"Jesus," Hunt said, expelling a low, slow breath. "Every now and then, I think I've seen everything. Then I wait a few days, and shit like this happens." I found myself in a similar situation. My cases grew more challenging—and the perpetrators more depraved—the longer I worked. When I placated my parents and agreed to do this job, I thought it would be easy. Sit at my computer, hack into something, solve a crime, collect a check. Instead, I got to flex my hacking muscles, but I've also been shot at, forced to shoot a man myself, and gotten into more scrapes than I cared to count. Gloria's concern for me made sense.

Hunt's voice rooted me back in the present. "All right, I have the files up. Keep in mind everything about this Carter kid is preliminary."

"I understand," I said.

"The mother and son were killed by the same gun . . . a three-fifty-seven. Three slugs to the chest each." He squinted. "Any of them probably could have been fatal."

"What about Andre Carter?"

"Three slugs to the chest."

"Caliber?"

"Don't know yet," Hunt said. "Forensics has the bullets."

"How about Dante Johnson, then?" I said. "Other than the three rounds, any signs of injury?"

After a moment of perusing a file, Hunt said, "Nothing recent, no. Looked like he broke his arm when he was a kid, but I didn't see anything else."

"No evidence he'd taken a beating?"

"A bad one?" I nodded. "No. If he did, his attackers were careful enough not to leave him with any signs for later. Why do you ask?"

I recounted my recent schooling on gang initiations. "If this kid were in a gang, he would have been physically inducted."

"Meaning they would have beaten the hell out of him."

"Basically."

Hunt shook his head. "It would leave marks. The body can only take so much pounding before injuries become obvious. I've seen what you're describing before. There are signs, even a few years later, in the bones. This kid didn't have anything like it."

Another check in the *Not in a Gang* column. "I suppose Andre Carter was the same?" I asked.

"I haven't finished my examination yet," said Hunt. "No obvious signs of past injury other than a scar on his leg, though. My guess is he got it ten years ago."

"When he was about eight or nine."

"Kids around those ages hurt themselves in about a

million different ways. He could have slipped and fallen on a soda bottle for all any of us know."

His mother should know. I didn't want to descend on her like some vulture reporter, however; I would try and talk to her at her son's viewing. "All right," I said. "Thanks, Doctor. I may come back if I need to run anything else by you."

"Now you value me as a physician?" he said with a brow raised.

"You're an unethical bastard. It doesn't mean I don't respect your medical opinion."

"Aren't you a charmer?"

"I have my moments," I said.

BY THE TIME I arrived home, I was ready to fall asleep. One can only take so much of talking to hookers and pimps, eating lousy food, and getting waylaid by men aptly named Tank in a single evening. Even I have my limits. I walked inside and trudged upstairs. Gloria woke up when I entered the bedroom. She rubbed her eyes, sat up, and showed a tired grin. "Late night with the hookers?"

I smiled. "Yes, actually. I don't know if I've ever been propositioned so much in my life."

"What if I proposition you?"

"I'm pretty sure you'll succeed where they failed," I said. I went into the bathroom and got ready for bed, changing into my usual sleeping attire of a T-shirt and gym shorts. When I came out, Gloria still sat on the bed.

"I'm hungry," she said.

We walked downstairs to the kitchen. I wasn't used to making or eating snacks at this hour, so I scanned cabinets and cupboards for appropriate fare. "How about chips and guac?" I said once I completed my survey.

"Sounds good," Gloria said, sitting at the table.

I mashed two avocados, added some fresh salsa—normally, I would chop the vegetables myself, but I made allowances for the late hour—along with salt and a pinch of lime juice. In a few minutes, we could enjoy a bowl of guacamole and a bag of tortilla chips. Gloria dove in. I grazed by comparison. The role reversal was complete.

"What did you find out?" she said after finishing a chip. I watched her dip the next one. Her guacamole-to-chip ratio was too low for my tastes.

"Very large men can be surprisingly stealthy and quick," I said, flexing my neck. I'd be sore for a couple days. "Plus a good bit on the gangs. I don't think the second kid was a banger, either."

"Second kid?" she frowned.

I filled her in on the details. "The ME shares my opinion," I added, "for whatever it's worth."

"What do you mean?"

"The police are probably going to investigate these as gang killings. It's the higher-probability play."

"You can do your own investigation, though," said Gloria.

"I can," I concurred, "and I plan to. I'm just not sure how much help I'll have from the BPD."

"How much help do you usually get?"

I smiled again. "Fair point," I said.

IN THE MORNING, I GOT TO WORK AFTER BREAKFAST and coffee. Normally, I might have gone for a run around Federal Hill Park. Maybe later. My late-night activities in the city would have to be enough excitement for now. Andre Carter, the latest shooting victim, showed no evidence of being a gangbanger. He lived in a rough area known for gunplay, battles over turf, and the like, but I saw no signs he was wrapped up in any of it. Like Dante Johnson, Andre was a good student in a neighborhood where such an achievement was rare. Both finished their freshman years at Morgan State and continued their academic successes. While a gang member going to college and earning good grades was possible, it struck me as improbable.

I contemplated two young men, both of whom lived in bad neighborhoods beset by violence, who got shot in ways normally reserved for red or blue-clad young criminals. Additionally, Anisha Johnson was gunned down outside the funeral home, an act of barbarism no one I talked to heard of happening before. Both Andre and

Dante went to Morgan, a historically black college in Baltimore. I wondered how difficult breaking into Morgan's student records would be.

Answer: not very. In my experience, most colleges only used slapdash security to protect their networks. Students' personal information was sometimes sectioned off on the network and harder to access, but the basics proved readily available. Even if Morgan used robust security, I felt confident I could get past it. I learned the science of computers in college and the art of compromising them both at home and in Hong Kong. I taught myself a lot as a teen, then learned a bunch more in China. I might still be there if the government hadn't found us, thrown me in jail for nineteen days, and given me the boot.

I didn't think data like social security numbers—what IT people and hackers called "personally identifiable information"—for either kid would be useful, so I stuck to the more traditional college data. Each pulled a GPA over 3.0 in their first years. Despite differing majors, they took one class in common—African-American Studies 101, taught by a Dr. Maurice Reid. They lived on campus in neighboring dorms and pledged different fraternities. Other than the three days a week one semester they shared a classroom, I couldn't even find any evidence they knew each other. The young men were Facebook friends—and shared other acquaintances on their lists—but barely interacted on the platform. They weren't connected on any other social media.

Two dead college kids. One dead mother. All looked like gang killings, but I harbored doubts as to whether any were. Little in common between the younger victims.

What the hell did I get myself into?

* * *

After a run and shower, I went back to work. I tried to reach Paul King at the station and his cell, but he didn't answer. Instead, I called Rich. "King mentioned he was working with you on something," he said.

"You didn't try to talk him out of it?" I asked.

"He wouldn't listen, anyway."

"I've learned a lot since I talked to King last. Now I don't think these two kids were in gangs."

Rich laughed in my ear. "Seriously?"

"What?"

"We have two kids shot. Each was wearing rival colors in the wrong part of town. And your brilliant theory is neither one was a banger?"

"It sounds a little flimsy when you put it in those words," I admitted.

"Because it is. If it walks like a duck, quacks like a duck—"

"It could also be a platypus."

"I don't think they quack," Rich said.

"I'll look for your zoology degree next time I visit you."

Exasperation crept into Rich's voice. This happened with some regularity when we talked. "Look. I know you love to be contrary. Sometimes, it pays off. But these are gang killings."

"You working King's detail now?" I said.

"No," said Rich. "I still work homicide, which both shootings were. I've heard tensions are running higher than normal, though. Our gang units are concerned there's going to be a spate of violence."

"If these were turf killings, wouldn't the spate have already started?"

"Everyone thinks these kids were bangers," Rich said after a sigh.

"Groupthink," I countered. "Hasn't the BPD gotten in trouble a couple times for being in lockstep? Maybe a different perspective is what you need."

Rich hung up on me.

Maybe I would peddle my different perspective to someone else.

* * *

MY PHONE VIBRATED on the nightstand. I glanced at the time: two-ten A.M. Caller ID told me it was Paul King. This couldn't be good news. "Hello?" I mumbled.

"Got two gang shootings," he said. "Real ones this time."

I pulled myself into a seated position. "Rich told you my theory?"

"Yeah. You just woke up, so I'll only say it's bullshit and spare you anything worse."

"Where are you?"

"At the scene. Poplar Grove and Riggs. You know it?"

West Baltimore. In the neighborhood Freddie Gray called home, if my geography were right. "Vaguely," I said. "I'm on my way."

"I'll alert the media," King said and hung up.

I threw on the clothes I shrugged out of last night, gargled with some mouthwash, and headed to the west side. I arrived to a gaggle of police cars on Riggs. Their blue and red lights bathed the neighborhood. A local news van joined the melee beside me. I got out of my car, showed my badge and ID to a uniform, and ducked under the yellow tape. King walked up to greet me. "First murder?"

"No," I said, "though I hope I don't have to make these visits regularly." I surveyed the scene. Two dead black men lay partially covered by sheets outside Rehoboth K&K Grocery. A third sat against the brick exterior, a pair of paramedics tending to his legs. Two windows in the corner store got shot out. Behind the grocery lay an alley, and the grass edging it was beset by weeds even in the fall. Rowhouses lined each side of the street past the alley, most in various states of disrepair. "What happened?"

"We don't know the whole story yet," King said. "Guy sitting there says he was taking a walk. The two dead guys ran into each other and drew down. He got caught in the crossfire."

"He going to be OK?"

"Took one in the calf. Ripped up some muscle, but it left without hitting the bone. He'll be fine. Coulda been a lot worse."

I moved closer to the corpses. Blood seeped through their clothes and into the white sheets. It lent the appearance of their chests being blanketed by red coverings. Age was never easy to determine, but I put both around sixteen to eighteen. Regardless, they were way too young to shoot each other to death. "Rich said gang violence is simmering," I mentioned when King stopped beside me.

He nodded. "This might be the first sign it's boiling over."

I let out a slow, deep breath. "A full-fledged war?"

"Maybe," King acknowledged.

"You think you can stop it?"

"After all the shit we've been through and the DOJ smackdown?" He shook his head. "No. Best we can do is clean up the bodies and throw anyone who survives in jail."

I didn't think such a strategy would be very effective, and I doubted whether King did, either.

A gang war. Great.

CHAPTER 5

Andre Carter was survived by his mother, Debi. After going home from the west-side crime scene and getting a few more hours of sleep, I rang her doorbell at 10:30. She lived maybe a mile from where I stood over two corpses last night. Both were around the age of her late son. None were old enough for their grisly fates. Debi Carter had a small rowhouse crammed in the middle of similar structures. The windows on some were boarded up. All were in need of some level of repair.

When she opened the door only wide enough to peek out at me, I said, "Miss Carter, I'm a private investigator." I showed her my ID. She rolled her eyes. "Erma Johnson hired me."

"Miss Erma?"

"You know her?"

"She's a sweet lady." Her voice was quiet, defeated. I didn't need to ask why.

"She hired me to look into the murders of her grandson and daughter," I said. "It seems the same thing happened to your son. I'm very sorry for your loss."

"Thank you," she said with a small bob of her head. "You want to come in?"

Inside needed as much attention as the exterior. Drab brown carpet covered the floor. The furniture looked like it came from a thrift store, and I doubted they would take it back in its current state. Walls screamed for fresh paint. Someone needed to clean up junk and recent food trash; I figured Debi had more important things on her mind than keeping a clean house. She sat on the sofa. Rather than risk a rickety chair, I took a seat at the other end.

"Thank you for seeing me," I said when we were situated.

Debi smoothed her black skirt. "Some policemen have come by," she told me. "A few reporters, too. I don't want to talk to none of them."

"I understand. I try to avoid both whenever I can."

She offered a token grin out of politeness. "You found anything?"

"The police think Dante and your son were in gangs—"

"My boy wasn't in one of them," she said. For the first time, conviction replaced the defeat in her voice.

"Erma Johnson said the same about her grandson," I told her.

"She's probably right."

"Anyway, the police have their theory. I've done some investigating. I don't think either one was in a gang."

"Of course not."

"The problem is," I said, "it would be easier if they were."

"What do you mean?"

"If they were gangbangers, the violence is understandable. They weren't. So why did they get shot, and why were they dressed like they were Pirates or Bucs when it happened?"

She let out a deep breath, but before she could answer, her phone rang. "It's my pastor," she said. She picked up and asked him to hold on a moment. "I can talk to you later tonight at the viewing. When you leave, you'll see a funeral home on the next street."

"I'll be there."

She told me the times, then went back to her call. I showed myself out.

* * *

PEOPLE FILED into the building as I drove into the parking lot. I saw one marked police car near the entrance and an obvious unmarked one farther back. Considering the funeral home shooting at the genesis of this investigation, I expected a larger BPD presence. I parked the Caprice near the detective's car and got out. On my way toward the funeral home, I patted my side, making sure the 9-millimeter was still holstered under my suit jacket. I tend to prefer a .45, but the bulk of it would interfere with the hang of my jacket. My suits are far too good to be compromised by a bulky gun. We all need to make sacrifices.

A uniformed officer stood at the door, eyeing everyone who walked in. He didn't try to stop anyone, nor did he say anything. He looked at me long enough to conclude I wasn't a serial killer, then his eyes passed to the couple walking in behind me. Another uniform stood in the lobby, and a third was stationed at the door to the viewing room. None of them moved or said a word. They would occasionally smile or incline a head to confirm they weren't statues or wax sculptures.

I nodded to the uniform at the viewing room door as I walked in. He didn't recognize me, though I'd seen him in Rich's precinct a few times. Speaking of my favorite cousin, I saw him talking to a well-dressed man near the casket. The expansive viewing room, at least twenty by forty feet, filled with people. Most of them were probably friends and family of the victim, but I also recognized a few local politicians. I imagined their disappointment at the lack of photo ops; not a single reporter came to the viewing. Selfies with mourners would have to suffice.

I walked to the guestbook and added my name to the many who signed it before I did. Rich finished talking to the man in the sharp suit, so I made my way to him. "Pastor," I said, offering him my hand.

"Good evening," he said, shaking my hand in a powerful grip. He was a dark-skinned black man about my height but a little wider. He looked like he could have played football in college. "Are you a friend of the family?"

"Not really. I'm a private investigator. Dante Johnson's grandmother hired me."

"That poor family," he said, shaking his head. "To lose two people so young . . . it's really a shame. What did you say your name was?"

"I didn't, but it's C.T. Ferguson."

He frowned in a thoughtful pause. "I think I've heard of you."

"I hope so. I'd hate to think I spent all that time talking to reporters for nothing."

He showed an easy smile. "I'm Pastor Webster, but you can call me Kevin."

"All right, Kevin. Did both the Johnsons and the Carters attend your church?"

"Yes, for years. I've known Dante and Andre since they were in elementary school."

"Did they know each other well?"

"They were acquaintances and friendly, but I don't know if I'd say they were friends."

"Both young men were found dressed in gang colors. Were they—"

"No," he said, cutting me off. "Not a chance."

I nodded. "I'd come to the same conclusion. Do you know anyone who would want us to think both young men were in them?"

Kevin sighed and shook his head. "No, I can't think of anyone. I know some boys in the gangs, of course. I've talked to them, tried to show them the church is better to belong to." He shook his head again. "Not many of them listen, though. Gangs offer tangible things faster."

"I'd like to talk with Andre's mother tonight."

"I'm not sure it's a good idea."

"Don't worry, Kevin. I know what it's like to bury a loved one before it's time. I'll be delicate."

He bobbed his head—not that I needed his approval —and I walked away. Thoughts of my sister Samantha, dead twelve years now, fluttered into my mind. I took a deep breath and focused on why I came tonight. A crowd of well-wishers surrounded Debi. I stopped at the photo table. Andre Carter had been an active kid, playing base-ball and basketball, earning a couple trophies in each sport. I also saw pictures of him in school plays, receiving academic awards, and at his graduation. Andre did a lot and did it well. His profile did not overlap with a gang-banger's. So who wanted to make him look like one, and why?

Rich joined me as I stood at the photo table. He wore a nice suit, but the fit and color may as well have announced he was a cop. I wondered if he wore the same one to work earlier. Rich's clothing regimens can't be disturbed. "What are you doing here?" he said.

"I could ask you the same thing," I said, cementing my status as the man of a million comebacks.

"We want a police presence here, considering what happened last week."

"Aside from the three uniforms, it explains the unmarked but obvious car, and the other plainclothes guy in the room."

"The other one?"

"Standing like a wallflower near the corner." I hitched my head toward a man in his forties across the room, trying to look interested in his cup of water while surveying everyone around him. "Considering his suit looks cheaper than most, I'm guessing he's a cop, too."

Rich looked. "Yeah, he's O'Hearn."

"So you've come around to my theory?" I pressed.

He shrugged. "Merely putting in a little overtime." He paused while someone else took in the table. When the other fellow left, Rich continued. "You know your little theory raises as many questions as it answers."

"I'm still working on those."

"Any luck?"

"I wouldn't be here if I'd been having good luck." I said. "Anything new from the BPD?"

Rich shook his head. "Nothing."

Just then, Debi Carter approached and touched my forearm. "Mr. Ferguson?" she said, "I think I'd like to get some air."

"Very well," I said, giving her the best smile I could summon under the circumstances. She grabbed my forearm, and we walked away.

"I'll send a uniform out with you," Rich said.

* * *

Debi Carter and I stepped outside the funeral home. We didn't go anywhere in particular—just a lap around the exterior—but I got the feeling she needed a break from everyone inside. When she talked, her voice took on more energy and life, like a weight lifted from her shoulders.

"You said Miss Erma hired you?" she asked.

"She did."

"And you think my boy's death might be connected to Dante Johnson's?"

"Yes, I do," I said. We walked side-by-side around the perimeter of the facility, making sure to stay far enough away from smokers, well-wishers, and other stragglers outside. The uniform trailed a few steps behind us. He was a young stocky white guy who looked a day overdue for a shave and a month overdue for a haircut. Maybe he took his grooming tips from Paul King.

"Because of the gang colors?"

"Yes. The police are chalking it up to the usual turf wars. I'm not convinced."

"I hope you figure it out. I'd like to see justice—not just for me, but for Miss Erma, too."

"So would I," I said. I hoped I could live up to her expectations; I wasn't exactly off to a roaring start.

Debi Carter stopped at the edge of the grass, so I paused with her. She looked down at the lawn, then back up at me. "Would you mind holding my shoes?" she said.

"Holding your shoes?" I blinked a few times.

"Yes." A smile came over her face, the first real one I'd seen from her. "When I was a girl, we had a big yard, and I loved to run around in the grass barefoot. My mom would tell me my feet were going to turn green." She grinned again, more wistfully this time. "I want to walk in it again. I want to think about my mom and pray."

It all sounded charming in a folksy sort of way, if a little silly. "Sure, I'll hold your shoes," I said. The uniform gave me a funny look as Debi Carter unbuckled her black flats. I shrugged at him. Debi handed me her shoes. She still had pantyhose on, so she wouldn't be barefoot, but it was probably as close as she wanted to get at her son's funeral.

"I'll only be a few minutes," she said. "Thanks for putting up with me."

"Take your time," I said. She had recently lost her son. I never wanted kids, but if one of my parents had recently passed, I would want someone to accommodate my strange requests. When Samantha died, I didn't do anything like walk around in the grass barefoot. Instead, I sulked a lot, raided my parents' liquor cabinet, got in a couple of fights, and watched my grades spiral downward for the next two months. Even though I eventually recovered, doing something like traipsing in the grass would have been easier for everyone—me especially.

Debi Carter walked a circuitous route, speeding up and slowing down at random as she moved through the funeral home's large front lawn. She settled on a spot a few feet from the sidewalk with her back to me and the uniform. No one walked by, and light traffic normal for the nearby roads passed on all sides. She put her head back and looked up to the sky, then raised her hands as well. After standing in the pose for about ten seconds, she brought her hands together, folded them, and brought them in front of her body.

I watched as Debi bowed her head. She was too far away for me to hear, and I wondered what she said. Years ago, I learned prayers should always begin with thanks. If I were Debi Carter, I would struggle finding something to be thankful for. Maybe it explained why I could never make a regular habit of praying—if I had something to be thankful for, I knew the earthly reason it happened.

Cars drove by sporadically. The lane closest to the sidewalk was turn-only, which veered onto a side street. A blue Chevy Nova straight out of the 1970s moved from the middle lane to the right. It wasn't going very fast. I saw the passenger's window roll down about halfway. A black-sleeved and black-gloved hand held a large revolver out the window. I shouted for Debi to get down, but the sound of three rounds exploding through the quiet evening air drowned my warning. Debi Carter's body rocked with the impact of the slugs. I drew my gun and ran closer. The arm went back into the window as the car lurched forward. I took aim on the Nova as best I could and fired. I hoped to hit a tire, but instead, I put four bullets in the rear of the car, one of them shattering a taillight in an explosion of white and red glass.

The uniform ran from behind me with his pistol out. I strode past him to the body of Debi Carter. She'd been hit three times in the torso. I remembered a similar pattern on both her son and Dante Johnson. The marksmanship made it likely whoever shot also shot them. Debi's chest remained still, which I expected considering the amount of blood spilled out of her and into the grass. I put my gun away and cursed. The uniform joined me again. People would pour out of the funeral home any second now. The young officer looked at the body, his mouth agape. This could get bad quickly.

"Remember your training," I said.

"Right," he said after a second. "I'll secure the crime scene."

Rich ran out of the building, gun in hand. I saw him, and he saw me.

All I could do was shake my head.

* * *

I GAVE my statement to the cops. Rich and Captain Leon Sharpe stood nearby. It all felt very surreal, like someone else dictated what happened, and I watched on a flickering TV. I'd never seen anyone get killed in such cold blood before. I have a lot of pride, but not too much to say I felt shaken.

The detective who took my statement flipped his notebook shut and walked away. He told me his name, but I'd already forgotten it. I stared out into the sea of flashing red and blue lights. The parking lot emptied, the funeral home evacuated. Two kids were dead, and now both of their mothers were, too. What did the families have in common? Was someone targeting them? I needed to see if there was anything there. Leon Sharpe approached me. His expression looked softer than usual, almost sympathetic.

"You all right?" he said. Sharpe stood a good four inches taller than me and outweighed me by at least seventy pounds. He looked like he reported for duty after bench-pressing a car and sacking the quarterback three times. His bald black head never betrayed a hint a single hair ever grew out of it.

I gave a slow nod. "Getting there."

"No tag number on the car?"

"No rear plate." I replayed the scene in my head. The gun hand went back into the window. The car accelerated. I fired at the tires. Four rounds slammed into the rear of the Nova on either side of the absent license plate.

"You sure?"

I rolled my eyes. "Do you really think I'm playing it fast and loose right now after what just happened?"

"You tell me." Sharpe narrowed his eyes and leaned in.

"How about I tell you to fuck off?" I said, then turned and walked away.

"C.T.!" Rich called after me. I heard him jogging to catch up.

"He deserved it."

"Maybe. Hell, even I think you're playing it straight now."

"Thanks . . . I think."

"You did fire into the street, though," he said.

"I hit the car."

"With every shot?"

"Yes," I said. "I batted a thousand, for all the good it did. Nobody died, except Debi Carter."

"This time," said Rich. "You can't just shoot at a car speeding off. Sharpe seems willing to look past it, but if you keep telling him to fuck off, he may not be."

"Fine. Next time, I'll tell him to go to hell."

Rich sighed. "Just take it easy, will you?"

"Yeah," I said. "I'll be sure to think about the captain's feelings when I'm trying to figure out who killed four people."

"You think the same person killed them all?"

"There's more than one person involved. Someone drove the Nova while the shooter opened fire."

"True," Rich acknowledged. "Let me know if you come to any conclusions, will you?"

"Don't I always?" I said.

Rich gave me a look. I walked away.

I had a lot of work to do.

CHAPTER 6

Two dead kids. Two dead mothers. On top of it all, gang violence in the city was boiling over.Their war wasn't my problem to solve, but if I could decipher what happened to the two families, maybe I could resolve everything. Until the next time someone wandered onto opposing turf in the wrong colors, at least. In Baltimore, reprieves were temporary.

Gloria called. I sent it to voicemail. I needed to dive into what Dante Johnson and Andre Carter shared in common. If I couldn't find much there, I'd look into their mothers. The two biggest commonalities were their neighborhoods and the college they attended. I'd already done some cursory digging into their records at Morgan. Now, I needed to go deeper. My last intrusion into Morgan's network showed Dante and Andre attended one class together: African-American Studies, taught by Dr. Maurice Reid.

The syllabus looked pretty basic. The course covered from the first slaves in North America through the end of the 1960s, and students who desired Dr. Reid's take on more modern times were told to enroll in the second-semester class. I spent six years in college, took classes from professors who wrote their own textbooks, and dealt with plenty of instructors whose ego filled any empty desks in the room. Dr. Reid topped them all. Each page of the voluminous syllabus featured at least one plug for his expertise, speeches, or books.

If he was so keen on promoting himself, I would oblige him by investigating. Reid earned his Ph.D. from Coppin State—another local historically black college—ten years ago. Since then, he spent a couple years there and the rest at Morgan. Self-promotion came easily to him, and I found a lot of material to comb through. Reid loved making fiery speeches. I watched some highlights on YouTube. He possessed a good delivery, and his anti-gang message was clear and presented with plenty of fire. He also had a book, *African-American Struggles in Modern America*, available on all the major platforms.

I went back to Morgan's network. Basic student information proved easy to access. The schedules and calendars of professors did not present a challenge, either. Tomorrow, Reid scheduled a speech on campus for noon. It promised "tough talk on a post-Freddie Gray Baltimore, including on the blight of gang violence." I didn't know how packed a professor's talk would be on a Saturday, but the Robert and June Ferguson Foundation bought an advance ticket to be on the safe side.

I could hardly wait to hear what the good doctor professed.

* * *

I SHOWED up a few minutes early for the speech and parked in the closest spot I could find. Security guards stood outside the front doors to the lecture hall. The broad-shouldered guard who patted me down looked at my non-detective ID and waved me in. Inside, I saw more security staff roaming the lobby and still more inside the hall itself.

I grabbed a bottled water from a vending machine and walked into the auditorium. It looked more like a theater except no balcony seats. The stage could hold a play, and the number of seats would guarantee a good gate. I headed to the upper section, filled only halfway. I took a seat near the top and at the end of a row.

A hip-hop song I didn't recognize—it would include most of the recent ones, though I liked my chances in a quiz on the classics—played softly through the audio system. If someone were sitting next to me, we would have been able to have a conversation. I scanned the crowd for anyone dressed like a gangbanger and came up empty. Score one for security..

After a sound check and another couple songs I didn't know, a man in a suit emerged from behind the curtain at eight minutes after the hour. He was a light-skinned black man in a sharp gray suit with a matching vest, white shirt, and black tie. The suit fit him better than a common off-the-rack model. If they gave out programs at this thing, I might have known his identity. "Welcome to Morgan State University," he said. "For those who don't know me, my name is Dr. Benjamin Cameron, Vice-President for Academic Affairs. I hired Doctor Reid, so if you took one of his classes and didn't do well, it's my fault." Dr. Cameron paused for light polite chuckling from the crowd before he continued. "Before we bring Doctor Reid to the stage, the university has invited someone else to say a few words. You may know him as a columnist for *The Sun*. He's written extensively on gang issues, and the problem of violence in African-American culture and inner cities. And he's a graduate of Morgan State University." Dr. Cameron paused for more applause, this round louder. "Please give a nice Bear welcome to Jeremiah Gardner!"

I read some of Gardner's columns over the years. His conservative ideals made him a minority among his city, his fellow columnists, and the black community. Gardner came out from behind the curtain and shook hands with Dr. Cameron. His darker complexion contrasted handsomely with his lighter gray suit and a silver tie bright enough to require batteries. He walked to the microphone to a nice ovation, smiled, and waved to the crowd.

Gardner talked for about fifteen minutes. I sort of paid attention, but I didn't come to see him, so my mind wandered back to the case. Gardner wasn't going to provide much in my pursuit. The parts of his talk I listened to were at least interesting. His opinion on gangs mirrored Reid's, though his resolution lacked Reid's sense of promised apocalypse.

After Gardner left the stage—to less applause than greeted him—Dr. Cameron came back out. The two men did a quick handshake as they passed and Cameron kept walking to the microphone. "I'd like to thank Mr. Gardner for giving us some of his time this afternoon. Now, I'm going to bring out the man you all came to see. He's a professor of African-American studies, a man frequently published in magazines and a recognized expert on inner cities and gang violence. Please give it up for Dr. Maurice Reid."

Reid got the biggest ovation of the day. About a quarter of the people in attendance stood and applauded. He wore a snazzy blue pinstriped suit I would have been proud to claim as one of my own. He paired it with a pristine white shirt and a red tie with thin blue stripes. Reid smiled and gave the crowd a few waves as he walked back and forth on the stage. He took the microphone out of its stand and kept pacing. As a short man, it took him a good number of strides to go from one end to the other. Reid possessed a medium complexion and short black hair graying at the temples.

From his constant motion and easy rhetoric, I got the feeling the professor could win over any crowd. He was assured of a future in politics if he wanted it. For the first part of the speech, I divided my attention between the crowd and him. I wanted to gauge their reactions, especially if it looked like any of them would react violently. No one did. I half heard what the good doctor said, and it sounded much like what I already read.

"My friends," he continued after a few opening remarks to prime his audience, "I teach a lot of people every semester at Morgan State." A few cheers went through the crowd at the mention of the college. "I teach one history class, and three courses specifically on African-American history and culture. You know by now we recently lost two young men who went to this school. They were cubs in a college of Bears. It was my privilege to educate both Andre and Dante on the great history and culture of our people. Anyone who knew them will know they were dedicated students. They asked questions, they were bright, and they were eager to learn." Reid paused. The crowd applauded as he turned away and took a deep breath.

"To lose such fine young men to the plague of gang violence is a terrible shame," Reid went on. "It is a scourge, a blight upon our city. How many more young men . . . old men, women . . . will we have to lose before we decide enough is enough?" Reid's small frame belied the power of his voice. The microphone helped, but his baritone would fill a lecture hall unaided. The crowd sat transfixed. "The gangs don't own Baltimore. They may think they do, but they don't. This is still our city, my friends. It's a city full of good, hardworking people—the kind of people who go to their job every day, raise their children, and go to church. Be sad. Mourn the loss of Andre, of Dante, and of their mothers. Feel it in your hearts . . . but I also want you to steel yourselves. The gangs are getting out of control. It's only a matter of time before their violence consumes them. Maybe then, we can have our city back. Until then, keep strong, my friends, and keep the faith.

"I know what you're thinking—keeping the faith is hard. We tried to keep the faith after Freddie Gray. We tried again when the cops who killed him got off." Murmurs and boos went up. Reid kept going. "Gangs are taking over our neighborhoods, and we watch it happen. Black, white, young, old doesn't matter. We're enablers. If we don't fight back, that's all we're doing: we're enabling these bastards to come in and take control of our neighborhoods. It's happened for too long here and plenty of other places. And I'm tired of it. I'm tired of it!"

Several people shouted, "Tired!" when Reid punctuated his point. This speech felt like it was shifting to a preacher giving a favorite sermon to the congregation. "People have seen what the gangs can do," Reid said. "They've heard about the random and wanton acts of violence at the Inner Harbor. That's a place filled with tourists and police. If the gangs can wreak havoc there, what stops them from doing it somewhere else?" Reid paused, almost like he expected someone to answer his question. "Nothing. Nothing stops them. Not the threat of arrest, not the fear of the police, and certainly not the fear of the people.

"My friends, it's time to change it all." Applause started in short bursts, but never built because Reid kept talking. "It's time to change it. This country was founded on the principle that we the people can do it. We elected a president—a *black* president—twice based on the principle of 'yes we can.' I'm here today to tell you we the people can take our neighborhoods back from the gangs ruining them." This time, Reid paused for the applause. He allowed himself a smile as he looked over the crowd. Here was a man in his element. "It won't be easy, and it won't happen overnight, but we can do it. Yes, we can. Yes, we can." Reid and the crowd both chanted the refrain for a solid minute.

"I'm not going to give away how to do it now," Reid said once the chant died down. "I'd have to talk until I was hoarse, and you'd have to take a lot of notes." The audience laughed. "But I do have a new book coming out." Another round of applause started. Reid tried to corral it with a few hand waves, but it continued, and he waited for it to end before talking again. "I've been working on the book for a while now. This is a topic not unique to Baltimore, though our problem is closest to my heart. Many cities face problems like ours. In the book, I talk about what the city government can do, and more importantly, what people like you and me can do in our own neighborhoods to take the streets back from those who stole them from us."

More applause went up, and Reid basked in this newest round. I couldn't be surprised at news of another tome hitting the shelves. If any idiot with an Internet fad could get a book deal, someone with the credentials and charisma of Maurice Reid should have publishers fighting over his next manuscript. Good for Reid. His message sounded angry and held potential to cause more violence, but it was a message more people should hear. Turning his speech event into a glorified plug struck me as kind of cheap, though.

I didn't want to hear any more ads for his book. I left the auditorium, got in my car, and drove home.

Doctor Reid just became a lot more interesting.

* * *

For a published author with such a natural gift of gab, Maurice Reid's detailed history was lacking. I conducted cursory research on him before. Now, I probed deeper. The problem was Reid's background lacked depth. He could fill a ledger book with things from the last dozen years. Before then, however, he made barely a peep in any context. High school diploma. Bachelor's degree. One credit card. An apartment and a car, the same of both for many years. Only the very basics. Some people lived like this, but I smelled something fishy.

My good friend Joey Trovato is an expert at two things: eating and creating new identities for people. The order of Joey's proficiencies depends on his appetite, but he's been in the ID business much longer than I've worked as a private investigator. I frequently sought his opinion in my cases, and all it cost me was the considerable expense of a meal with an Italian of boundless appetite. I didn't want to bust in on Joey's vacation, however, so I tried to apply maxims he taught me. One of the first was a spotty history past a certain number of years was a likely sign of a fake. Most background checks only went so far. Clearance investigations peaked at ten years. A decade of made-up history was enough to fool most people.

I tried my damnedest not to be most people.

Where was Reid's history beyond the twelve-year mark? I checked the high school he claimed to have graduated from twenty-six years ago. The friendly lady in the office told me they had no record of a Maurice Reid or anyone else with a variety on spelling his last name even attending around the listed time. Another woman at the small southern college Reid supposedly got a degree from from told me the same thing, except with a drawl making me yearn for sweet tea. I could have looked further but didn't see the point. Reid was oh-for-two so far. The swings and misses would only get worse the more I probed.

Instead, I focused on the recent events. Reid legitimately earned his doctorate degree, though now I wondered how closely Coppin scrutinized his undergrad work. Morgan seemed happy with him; they certainly wrote about him and trumpeted his appearances and speeches sufficiently. His students held more mixed opinions. Interestingly enough, both Dante Johnson and Andre Carter left Reid negative reviews on Ratemyprofessor.com. They both mentioned his love for hearing himself talk. Having been to a speech, I could confirm it.

Earlier, I found Reid's talk by checking his university calendar, but I only looked a day ahead. Now I checked the upcoming weeks. Tomorrow, Reid ran a support group for people and families affected by gang violence. The schedule showed it running twice a week. Maybe I would need to alter my opinion of Reid—after all, shameless self-promoters rarely involved themselves in helping people.

I added the support group meeting to my calendar. Might as well check it out in person.

CHAPTER 7

The support group met in the basement of a church I never recalled driving past. Holy Redeemer Church, especially with its very generic name, didn't stand out in any way. It lacked the steeple and spires which lent churches their distinctive look and appeal. This one could have been a retail store in a past life. It was a one-story building with a flat roof, double doors in the front, and large windows designed to show off what was inside. All it needed was the rest of the attractions in a strip mall. I could have used the obligatory Chinese restaurant.

The basement where the meeting took place was an odd fit with the rest of the place. The stairs were narrow and I had to duck as I got closer to the bottom. The ceiling was about three inches over my head. Anyone who stood six-four and wore shoes would be in trouble. The walls needed paint; in some spots, bare drywall showed through. One large room dominated the lower level and a hallway bisected it and led around a corner.

I felt weird walking in, as if I were invading some

kind of sacred place. I never felt it when breaking into a house or office or hacking into someplace I didn't belong. Selective morality is a wonderful thing. The people in this group needed to be here—or they thought they did, or someone told them they did. I never attended a support group before. It had been suggested to me after my sister died, but I never went. The shrink my parents insisted I see proved dreadful enough.

As I entered, I saw a table to the right topped with a fresh-smelling pot of coffee, tea bags, and accessories for both along with a box of donuts and a bowl of apples. I thought about taking an apple and making some tea. On the one hand, I already felt out of place. On the other, I needed to look like I belonged. If you're an interloper, looking like you belong can make a lot of difference. Besides, I hadn't eaten in a while.

I heard a couple of voices nearby, but I was the only person in the main room. I walked across the drab tiled floor to the chairs, which were arranged in a semicircle. No chair set apart from the rest. I guess the arrangement aimed to make group members feel Reid was one of them.

Someone else arrived and helped himself to coffee at the refreshment table. He was a tallish thin black man who looked to be in his early fifties. He wore dark blue jeans and a gray sweater. The sweater showed a hole in the left elbow. I sat in a chair far from the center of the semicircle. The latest arrival grabbed a donut to go with his coffee and crossed to the chairs. He walked slowly and didn't look up. I wondered if everyone would look as unhappy as he.

I stood and nosed around the area. An office was situated down the hallway. A sign promised restrooms around the corner, and I encountered a second door to the office there. A few more people wandered in as I walked back to the chairs and sat to wait. I noticed no one looked up or socialized much. Feelings of being an intruder crept upon me again, and I fidgeted in my seat. Reid walked in from the office, a smile on his face. A man I hadn't seen before followed him. He was much taller and broader than Reid and looked like he could win a wrestling match with an alligator. "How is everyone tonight?" Reid said, smiling and clapping his hands.

The assemblage murmured but didn't put much into their collective response. I stayed quiet in the hopes I wouldn't have to say anything. Stories of AA meetings were full of people who were only comfortable listening. Reid and the other man took their seats; the stranger plopped down next to me, while Dr. Reid sat four chairs away.

"I hope everyone has had a good week," Reid said. "I'm here tonight so we can all share our stories, our pain, and our personal victories." He smiled again, and this time one man and one woman joined him. It was an improvement. "Before we begin, though, it seems introductions are in order. We have someone new with us tonight." He looked at me. "Welcome to the group."

"Thank you," I said.

"What's your name?"

"Trent." I typically gave people my middle name in situations like this. It's less distinct and far less embarrassing than my first name. I have good reason to go by my initials.

"Trent, I'm glad you could come out with us tonight. My name is Dr. Maurice Reid. We're all on a first-name basis here, so you can call me Maurice. The man sitting next to you helps me run this group. His name is Calvin. Going around to your right, we have Jackson, Elizabeth, Chris, Andre, Brent, and Keisha." I got murmured greetings and small smiles from all of them. "Why don't you tell us a little about yourself?"

"I'm twenty-nine," I said. It was probably the last truth I would tell for a while. "I live downtown and work there, too . . . in finance. On nice days, I ride a bike to work."

"All right. We have a rule, Trent. On your first night, you have to share your story. Some groups let you listen indefinitely. I've found hearing other people talk isn't helpful by itself. So how has gang violence affected you?"

My mouth went dry.

* * *

"Trent?" Reid said when I lapsed into silence.

"It's all right," Elizabeth offered in encouragement. "Sharing on your first day is hard. Take your time."

Time was exactly what I needed. I didn't have a story to share here. The closest I got to gang violence was working this case. A dozen eyes stared at me. I debated the wisdom of coming here. Reid would count as a person of interest but what about everyone else? Here I sat surrounded by people with probable cause to hate gang members, led by a man who talked about them with fire and brimstone. Whoever killed my four victims could be in this room. I needed to devise something.

"My sister died when I was sixteen," I blurted out. It was true, though a heart problem caused her death.

"What happened?" Doctor Reid said. He leaned forward and rested his chin on his right hand.

"I was away on a school trip. My sister went to college, got really good grades, was involved in campus clubs. She had an activist streak in her . . . hated war and violence. She and some of her friends were in a club for it, I think." All true so far. Now, however, the lies needed to take over the tale. "One night, they were out downtown, and she got hit by a gangbanger's stray bullet." I paused. I was committed to the story now and needed to keep going. The familiar pain of my sister's death squeezed my chest. The first tears pooled in my eyes.

"That's terrible," Elizabeth said.

I nodded. "Like I said, I was away at the time, so I didn't know what had happened. I got a call telling me my sister died. It wasn't until I turned eighteen when my family told me what really happened."

"You must have felt terrible," Reid said. Wood creaked as Calvin's hands gripped the armrests of his chair.

"Angry, mostly," I said. "My sister was still dead." I felt a few more tears well, and one slid down my right cheek. I wiped at it with my hand. Despite making things up on the fly, I gave these people an amount of truth I hadn't expected to provide. I ended up tapping a real vein of emotion.

"How did you react when you learned the truth?"

I took a deep breath and dabbed at my eyes. "Silence," I said. "I couldn't say anything. I always suspected foul play involved with her death, but to hear about it after the fact was just . . . I don't know, insulting, I guess. I may have been sixteen, but I could have handled the truth."

"Whatever happened to the gangbanger?" Dr. Reid asked.

"I don't know," I said. "I tried looking up news stories to see what I could find, and there's nothing out there. He's as anonymous now as he was before he pulled the trigger." I paused and dabbed at my eyes again. My tight chest needed a breath or two. "I hope he's dead, though."

Dr. Reid gave a subtle nod. Everyone else looked at me, so they didn't notice. I glanced at Calvin. He looked down as soon as I did. He shook his head and inflicted a white-knuckle grip on the arms of the chair. His breaths sounded deeper than mine, and I harbored good reason to be taking deep breaths.

"How do you feel now?" Reid said.

"A little better, I guess," I said. "Getting it out there is bound to help, right?" I wiped at my eyes again. If I thought I would adapt the story of my sister's death for this support group, I would have brought a handkerchief. Or four. Or considered not coming at all.

"That's right, and that's what we're here for."

I nodded. The tears didn't stop. Even thirteen years later, my sister's death felt like a brass-knuckled punch to the ribs.

"If you need the restroom, it's down the hall to the right."

"Probably a good idea." I got up and walked down the corridor and around the corner. The second office door was on my right. I walked past it and into the men's room. I ran cold water and splashed it on my face. After a few slow, deep breaths, the tightness in my chest eased. My brain stopped replaying the night I learned about Samantha's death on a continuous loop of misery. I sloshed more water on my face, then wiped it off with paper towels.

The office. I could probably get a member list from there. The group would expect me to be gone a few minutes.

I rarely needed so much time.

* * *

The office was dark when I walked in. I couldn't turn the light on without alerting everyone to my presence. An ugly L-shaped desk chewed up much of the square footage. I wiggled the mouse, and the computer woke up. The monitor offered some illumination. In addition, it showed me the computer wasn't password-protected. This would be easy, which was always a good thing when limited by time.

Compounding the simplicity was a file on the desktop titled "Member Roster.docx." It always amazes me when people leave valuable files on their desktops. Even a middling hacker could find them elsewhere, but raising the difficulty also makes things take longer. Sometimes, the clock is the biggest factor working against an attacker. Leaving important files in obvious places was a recipe for disaster.

A large HP printer occupied one end of the desk. It looked a few years old, and the dust on it told me Reid didn't use it often. If the printer were noisy, everyone would know I went into the office. Instead, I opened the Word file and snapped a picture of it with my phone. I closed the document, set the computer to sleep again, and walked out via the door I entered.

"How are you, Trent?" Reid asked when I rejoined the group.

"Better now," I said. "Thanks."

"Did this help?"

"I think I got what I needed," I said.

CHAPTER 8

THE SUPPORT GROUP MEETING BROKE UP JUST AFTER three o'clock. A few people lingered and talked among themselves. I already felt like an interloper, and I lied in a spot where most people told their darkest truths. Sticking around to make small talk would have been rubbing salt in a nearly-healed wound. Instead, I drove home, changed into athletic attire, and went for a run around Federal Hill Park. Running always invigorated me, and I especially loved doing my laps here. Between the streets of Federal Hill and a stunning view of the Baltimore Harbor, this was the best spot.

I used the few blocks' walk back to my house as a cooldown. It was Saturday afternoon, so I passed people milling about and saw cars navigating the streets. Two doors slammed closed somewhere behind me. I thought I heard footsteps moving with some alacrity in my direction. I held my phone up as a mirror, and it showed me a man about to take my head off with his arm.

If I didn't get the warning, he probably would have knocked me out. As it was, the advance notice allowed me a half-second to duck, and his attempt to clothesline me from behind deflected off the top of my head. It still knocked me off balance—not to mention, hurt—but I wasn't splayed out on the sidewalk. I recovered from my stagger, put a few more steps between me and my assailant, and turned to see he wasn't alone.

Assholes always bring friends. Standing before me were two black men dressed in jeans, nondescript black hoodies, and red bandannas. Pirates. The one who hit me was the bigger of the two, though both were taller, brawnier, and younger. These weren't the goons I was used to squaring off against. I hoped they were untrained. "Recruiting drive?" I said.

"What?" the smaller one said.

"Don't get me wrong. I'm flattered. It's nice to be asked. But I don't think I'm Pirate material."

"We ain't recruiting you," the big one growled. "We just wanna see you bleed."

"I hope you're better fighters than talkers," I said.

They both advanced. Lesser-trained adversaries tend to come one at a time. These two followed a plan. I frowned. The big one smiled like a wolf upon finding an injured sheep. The other one, to my left, was about a step closer to me. His hands were open. The larger man balled his right hand into a fist which looked like it could dent a bank vault. An idea sprang into my head about how they were trying to do this.

Sure enough, the foe on my left tried to grab me. I resisted but only a little. The big one drew his fist back. I reversed the grip the other one held on my arm and pulled him directly into the path of a wallop. His head spun around as far as his neck would allow, and he was out before he hit the concrete.

"Treat all your friends like Bucs?" I said to the larger one remaining on his feet.

He yelled and threw a wild haymaker. Long arms like his take a while to connect on such a blow. I dodged. Another telegraphed punch met the same result. He kept trying them, and I kept stepping to the side or back. He came close to connecting a couple times, but before long, the punches slowed. Even someone in good shape can only go all-out for so long. I still didn't want to put my face in the path of a fist, but my opponent was laboring. I heard his breathing over the blood rushing in my ears.

More wild swings served as the only answer I would get. I let him throw a few more and suck wind even harder before I went on the offensive. I blocked one of his blows, then gave him a hard right cross in the solar plexus to cause serious gasping. I hit him with a few good body shots to bend him over, then planted a kick under his chin, snapping his head back and sending him to the ground.

I turned. The first asshole stirred and pushed himself up to all fours. I kicked him hard in the face, flipping him onto his back and giving him a return trip to dreamland.

While my two foes were out cold, I snapped their pictures. Before I could think of a clever hashtag to gloat about my victory on Instagram, sirens drew closer. It always surprised me when people called the police in Baltimore, and today was no exception.

Officers Brennan and Maine were first on the scene. Maine radioed for an ambulance while Brennan approached me, notepad in hand. "Where's Jennings?" I said, inquiring about his usual partner.

"Vacation," Brennan said. He was a jovial-looking Irishman with blond hair and a strawberry blond goatee. Like me, he probably struggled to grow facial hair beyond it. The curse of Irish blood. "What happened?"

"Two Pirates decided they didn't like me," I said. "I can't imagine why."

"Yeah, I'm sure everyone loves your personality." He jotted a few things.

"Why don't they issue you tablets?"

Brennan snorted. "Shit. No money for one thing. We've had to do a lot of retraining and buy body cameras after the DOJ kicked our ass. Even if we had the scratch, some asshole would just steal them, anyway."

Before either of us could say anything else, my phone rang. I answered it while Brennan frowned at the interruption. "C.T., you'd better get down here," said Rich.

"What now?" I asked.

"Gang shootings." He gave me the location. "I know you have a theory about all this, but these two are legit. A Buc and a Pirate. Tit for tat."

This reminded me of the call Paul King made a few nights ago. The scene would probably be similar. "I'll be there soon," I said and hung up. "Gotta go, Brennan. Here's my statement: they attacked me. I defended myself well because I always do. The end."

"I might need more," he said. "Where are you going?"

"Gang shooting."

"Shit."

"Yeah," I said.

* * *

I PULLED up behind a row of police cars on Poplar Grove Street. I could tell from a few blocks away this would be a bad one. Red and blue lights flashed from down the street. Only as I got closer and the lights grew smaller could I really see the scene. Four patrol cars, two unmarked cars, an ambulance, and the medical examiner's truck sat outside a barrier of yellow tape. So did a bunch of people straining to see what went on.

I got out of the Audi and showed my ID to the uniform who stood guard at the perimeter on this side. He nodded and waved me in, so I ducked under the yellow tape. As the gathered throng of cops, paramedics, and medical examiners parted, I saw three bodies on the ground. Rich only mentioned two. I wondered what happened between his phone call and now. The sheet covering the closest corpse was equal parts white and red. Rich saw me and started talking as he approached. "Another gang shooting," he said. "I heard you saw one the other night, too."

"King tell you?" His head bobbed. "I'm still sticking to my theory on the Johnson and Carter cases."

"Not this one. We got another real gang shootout." He pulled the covering back. A dead black kid of about seventeen lay on the asphalt, his eyes closed. "The victim you're looking at is Dominique Barnes, and his street name in the Bucs is Iceman."

"Do we need to call Maverick and Goose in for questioning?"

Rich rolled his eyes. "This is a legit gang killing, C.T."

"What else went on?" I said. "You mentioned two bodies when you called, but I see three. It's not like you to be off by fifty percent."

"Yeah," Rich said with a wince. "A bystander got hit, too. He was alongside a house at first, so we didn't see him until he staggered out and fell in the street."

"Shit. An innocent caught in the crossfire." The last scene I went to had one, also, though the man there escaped serious injury. This fellow was not so lucky.

"Bound to happen."

I knew it was, but I didn't have to like it, and I couldn't be so matter-of-fact about it. It wouldn't bother me if the gangs wanted to go into an abandoned warehouse, stand in two long lines, and blast away at each other. The problem was it was never so clean and simple. Sometimes innocent people wandered into the path of a bullet meant for some asshole in a bandanna. In other cases, kids got gunned down to attribute the shootings to the gangs, then their mothers met the same fate, for reasons (and by persons) currently unknown.

We walked about fifty feet to the next body. I watched the crime scene technicians go over every inch of the asphalt. They flittered from one casing to the next to a cigarette butt to anything helping piece together recent events. The team looked like they were drowning in chaos, but their movements were quick and efficient.

"This is John Artis," Rich said as we looked down at the second victim. He looked even younger than the first. "His name in the Pirates is A-Train."

I shook my head, both at the terrible street names and the deaths of two teenagers. "It looks like they got the message," I said.

"You're really still skeptical the gangs killed those two kids and their mothers?"

"I am."

"Why?" Rich said. "Why would someone kill four people and make it look like the Bucs and Pirates did it?"

"To start a gang war," I said.

"To what end?"

"I don't know." I sighed. "I hack into things. Sometimes, I punch people in the face. I don't . . . start street battles."

"You might need a new theory," Rich said.

"Yeah," I said. "I just might."

BACK HOME, after confirming no more gangbangers lay in wait, I got back to work. The support group meeting didn't tell me much about Dr. Reid. I got the impression he took the group seriously and wanted to help the people who came. He was still a self-important blowhard with a murky past. At least, I could forgive him the self-important part. No one else at the session sparked my interest except Calvin. His white-knuckle chair grips and scowls during my story showed a lot of anger.

Maybe enough anger to kill.

The member list I took a picture of showed him as Calvin Terrell. I hunted around the BPD for information. Four results popped up for the name, and I eliminated the obvious mismatches until only the fellow from last night remained. Calvin's mug shot glared back at me from my monitor. He didn't look any happier in it than he did at the meeting.

The unflattering photo came from the most recent of his four arrests. Four incidents of violence, three of which were against gang members. The first came when Calvin was only seventeen years old. He nearly beat a gang-banger to death. The second time he got popped, also for a violent assault, earned Calvin a ten-year prison sentence. He was out after four. Most recently, two decades after the initial incident, he was a person of interest in the death of Buc lieutenant, Jackson "Steel" Orr. No charges were filed, and the BPD listed the murder as unsolved.

I read the case file. Orr died twenty months ago, not far from the three corpses I saw earlier. He'd been shot.

Three times in the chest.

With a three-fifty-seven.

CHAPTER 9

ERC Construction owned a mid-sized building located amid a large yard in Catonsville, about ten minutes from Baltimore. The enclosure also held a warehouse, a few smaller storage sheds, some heavy equipment parked near the main building, and the usual detritus associated with the industry. The office manager showed me to Gary Lennox's office and told me he would be back shortly. I watched her walk away with some interest. She was short, probably just a shade over five feet, but she filled out her beige blouse and light blue jeans nicely. Her short brown hair stopped just after the collar of her shirt. She sat again at her desk and started working. I busied myself with looking around Gary Lennox's office.

It was small, almost as if someone measured the dimensions and hung the drywall around the furniture. Between the desk, chairs, and bookcase, there was barely room to walk. Turning around would require a year of gymnastic training. Two diplomas hung on the wall, one a bachelor's in mechanical engineering and the other an MBA. I wondered how many people who owned small construction companies could boast of these qualifications. The MBA was dated from sixteen years ago, likely putting Gary Lennox around forty. The man walking toward the office confirmed my guess. He was about my height but thirty pounds heavier and with a brawny build to match years of construction work. His black hair showed strands of white at the temples, and his goatee long ago succumbed to its own invasion of gray. Gary Lennox wore faded blue jeans, a tan polo shirt, and a pair of well-worn brown industrial boots.

He closed the door and looked at me. "You're the detective?"

"I am."

"Gary Lennox." He extended his hand.

I shook it. "C.T. Ferguson."

"What's this about?" He sat behind his desk, and I took a seat in one of the uncomfortable guest chairs. Mine were much nicer. On the other hand, I didn't have a bulldozer handy. All in all, probably a wash.

"One of your employees came up during a case I'm working on. I just wanted to find out some more about him."

"Can I see your ID?"

"Sure." I showed him my license and badge. He looked at them, squinted, peered again, and then nodded. "This is a sensitive case, so there is a need for discretion," I said. "Can we keep this chat between us?"

"Sure. What kind of case are you working on?"

"I really can't say."

"Some big corporation has its hooks in you?"

"Not even close."

Gary Lennox frowned. "All right. Whose name came up?"

"Calvin Terrell," I said. "What can you tell me about him?"

"Calvin? He's a good worker. He gets here when he's supposed to, works hard, supervises his crew well. His projects are always finished on time or ahead of schedule, and his workers really like him."

"Any personality conflicts or problems with violence?"

"No company has complete harmony among its employees."

"Anything you can tell me here would be helpful."

"You asked me for discretion," Gary Lennox said. "How far does that go on your side?"

It was a fair question. "I can't say I'll never repeat anything you tell me," I said. "But I will promise only the people who really need to know will learn any of this, and only when they need to know it."

Gary nodded. He must have found my discretion rules acceptable. Most people did. I didn't like the idea of people running their mouths about me, so I tried to minimize doing it to others, especially in the presence of law enforcement. Rich and I disagreed on this, but our opinions varied on a great many things in the policing arena. "Calvin would argue with people here and there," Gary said. "Nothing significant. Like I said, every company has it. He got into an altercation with another worker about four years ago, though."

"They got into a fight?" I asked.

"It was headed there, but others broke it up first.

They jawed at each other and did some shoving but nothing more."

"What happened after this incident?"

"I transferred the other man to a different crew," Gary said. I wondered if his MBA taught him such tactics.

"Do you know the guy's name?"

He let out a breath and thought. "Tyrone . . . something. Adamson, Tyrone Adamson."

I considered Calvin's BPD file. A bunch of names were in there, but Tyrone Adamson could not be counted among them. Nothing significant must have happened after their little shoving match. "What went down after you transferred the other guy?" I said.

"He quit not long after," Gary said. "Stopped showing up."

Interesting. "I think it's all I need. Thanks for your help."

"Sure," Gary Lennox said. We shook hands again. "I hope Calvin isn't involved in anything bad. I'd hate to lose him."

"Just doing some checking after his name came up."

"I hope that's all it ends up being."

"We'll see," I said.

* * *

I sat in my Caprice a few houses away from Calvin's. The car was an undefined shade of blue, and I acquired it during a past case where I had to work off the grid. Since then, I took it back to the "automotive reconfiguration engineer" who sold it to me and requested modifications.

I figured if I owned an ugly car, I may as well make it a useful one. Bullet-resistant glass replaced the standard Chevy offerings all around, and the body is close to bulletproof. All this work made the car a uniform color, at least, rather than the variations on a cyan theme it sported before. The added weight meant the stock V-8 got replaced by a more eager model. I wouldn't drive it into a nest of machine guns, but some asshole with a pistol would have a hard time hitting me if I sat in it.

Speaking of assholes with guns, Calvin hadn't come out or made a peep. While I waited, I used my phone to do a little more research on him. I made a secure connection to my computer at home, where all my traffic was anonymized and run through a virtual private network at least once. The Nova used in the shooting of Debi Carter didn't have a rear plate. Maryland law required one—and a matching one up front to boot—so driving without it constituted a risk.

Those who gun down women outside funeral homes may be less risk-averse than the average person, however.

It made me wonder if Calvin owned the car. Maybe he stole it, or someone else did. I checked his vehicle registrations. Like many other people in the country, he owned a Toyota Camry. It was the only car on file for him. Past records didn't turn up a Nova. Calvin's house featured a one-car garage, though, and I saw the Camry parked at the curb.

Either he was a hoarder or the Nova remained hidden behind the garage door. With no activity from the house, I kept digging. Calvin had a brother and sister, but neither owned a car of interest in their lifetimes.

A few minutes later, Calvin emerged from his house.

He got in the Camry and drove away. I waited for him to turn off the street plus another minute. Then I got to work. Dusk would provide me some cover from prying eyes. I put on thin black gloves and knocked on the front door. No dogs barked. I didn't see any alarm company signage.

Within a minute, thanks to the lockpicks on my special keyring, I opened the front door. Little natural illumination remained, and I didn't want to risk turning on a light and alerting the neighbors of my presence. Calvin kept a messy home. Even for a bachelor, he was a pig. Ignoring the shopworn living room furniture, plates, bowls, and utensils on the coffee and end tables, I encountered a few pizza boxes piled up in the kitchen. The general odor of the house told me they might not be empty.

Another door beckoned off the dining room, which was the neatest room in the house. Of course, its tidiness stemmed from its apparent total disuse. The layer of dust told me Calvin probably never sat at the table, let alone eaten a meal in here. As an unmarried man, I understood the appeal of eating in front of a nice TV—though Calvin's appeared a bit small by modern standards—but sometimes, everyone needs to eat in the dining room. The door opened into a dark garage. I saw the outline of a car and the bare interior walls.

I flipped the switch on. A blue Nova sat on the concrete. I walked around to the back. No rear plate was attached. Four bullet holes pockmarked the rear end of the car, and one of the taillights was missing.

CHAPTER 10

I took pictures of the Nova and walked back into the house proper. Calvin didn't seem to be in a hurry to return. I used this time to nose around his sty of a house. Confirming he owned the Nova was great, but I still wanted more. I saved the living room for the end and started in a spare bedroom Calvin turned into an office.

A cheap wooden desk with a mismatched hutch sat against the wall on the right. Completing the trashy look was a collection of printouts and Post-Its stuck all over. I read a few. They sounded like snippets of Dr. Reid's speeches. The attribution on one didn't match, however; it listed Malcolm Reedy as the speaker. I snapped photos of all the various notes. Calvin also left a book by this Reedy on the desk. *The Blight of Gang Violence: A Problem and a Solution*, dated thirteen years ago, sounded very much like something Reid would have penned.

I continued hunting but didn't uncover anything of interest. A .357 would have been a nice find. Either

Calvin took it with him, or he kept it well-hidden. I didn't want him to know I'd been here, which limited my searching to more gentle means. After looking out the window to confirm no one was around, I left via the front door and climbed back into my car.

Once seated, I reconnected to my server at home for another secure session. I uploaded the pictures I took, then invoked a script to run optical character recognition and search for the strings of text it found. Results soon appeared. The quotes were a mix, with some attributed to Malcolm Reedy and others to Maurice Reid. There were pairs of very similar sayings, one belonging to each man. Change a few words, plug in a new city, update the president to the current occupant of 1600 Pennsylvania Avenue, and a Malcolm Reedy quote morphed into a Maurice Reid talking point.

I researched the book I saw on Calvin's desk. It took a little digging, but I found an archived photo of Malcolm Reedy from fourteen years ago.

He bore an uncanny resemblance to one Doctor Maurice Reid.

Reedy's records stopped a dozen years ago when he went missing, though never declared dead. As far as I could tell, the Boston police never closed the case; they only stopped trying to solve it after a lengthy time. I got the feeling I could supply an answer for them.

A little more digging convinced me Reedy dropped off the grid and emerged a couple months later as Maurice Reid. The Internet was a Thing then, but the social media explosion wouldn't occur for a few years. People with phones didn't photograph, film, and upload their entire lives. Reedy's reinvention would be a lot harder today—at least without the help of a pro like Joey —but he pulled it off a dozen years ago.

The title of the book piqued my interest. What was the proposed solution? I didn't want to download the entire tome and give a couple dollars to its author. Within a minute, I found a journal article offering a detailed critique, and I pitied the author. Reedy's solution involved pitting gangs against one another on an ever-increasing scale. The occasional tit-for-tat shooting, he argued, did not rid the city of its problem quickly enough. He went on to posit tricking the gangs into escalation by pinning other murders on them.

Bingo.

More than a decade after Malcolm Reedy wrote those words, Maurice Reid got to put the plan into action with Calvin's help.

I saved all the information on my server and disconnected. Still no sign of Calvin. I didn't need anything else from him or his messy house, however. I drove home.

* * *

AN ALLEY RAN behind my house. Just off it, I recently installed a concrete parking pad. It fit both my cars—I usually moved the Caprice to the street when Gloria visited—and still left enough room in my small backyard for a grill. As usual, cars were parked sporadically on the alley, making navigating it an occasional adventure. I got out of the Caprice and locked the door. Footsteps came from somewhere behind me. I put my hand on my gun and started to turn.

"Don't do it," said a voice. I stopped. Something

jabbed into my lower back. "Why don't you gimme the gun? Nice and slow." I took it out of the holster with a two-fingered grip and handed it to my mysterious assailant. He snatched it and stuffed it into the waistband of his jeans. I hoped he would shoot his own dick off but no such luck. "We taking a ride. Let's go."

"In my car?" I said.

"Mine. In the alley." He nudged me with the muzzle, and I walked toward a late 'eighties Mustang GT. It was jet black with the silver 5.0 emblem on the side. Why have a five-liter V8 if you can't tell everyone about it? "You driving." He tossed me the keys. I got in. Whoever this guy was, he owned a classic Mustang with a five-speed manual. If it weren't for the whole gun thing, I might have liked him.

I hadn't started the car yet. "Where are we going?" I asked. I buckled my seatbelt and looked at my passenger. He was black, maybe twenty or so years old. He wore a blue shirt peeking from under the dark, nondescript hoodie. His face was long though not thin, and it combined with his small eyes for a sinister countenance. He looked a little taller than me when he walked past, and he was built like a basketball player. A baller who happened to have a nine-millimeter pointed at me.

"Head into the city," he said. He sat looking at me, turned about a quarter of the way toward my side. He hadn't buckled his seatbelt. When I started the car, the Mustang beeped to remind us he flouted the safety laws of Maryland. I declined to point it out to him.

I went down Riverside, then picked up Fort Avenue. I took it to Jackson, and then to Key Highway. Past Rash Field and around a sharp curve, Key Highway becomes

Light Street, which leads to Harborplace, and from there, any number of roads will take one anywhere in Baltimore. I followed Light to Calvert, then hung a left on Fayette, which was one way headed toward the west side. "You heading west," my passenger said.

"Figured it's where you were taking me," I said. "Or I was taking you. I'm not really sure who's taking whom here."

"Just drive."

"You could at least tell me why you came for me with a gun and have me driving somewhere."

"You a snoop working with the cops."

I wondered how he knew this. My interaction with Calvin happened as Trent the finance guy. Of course, two idiots threatened me recently. Ever since my picture made it into the paper—and online—after my first case, getting identified has been a risk. "Just because I'm a PI doesn't mean I'm your enemy," I pointed out.

"The police are," he said. "You working with them. That's enough."

"Even though I'm the one who figured out you were being played." We missed the light at Charles Street. When it turned green, I took a right. Years ago, my father taught me the lights in Baltimore were calibrated so a certain speed would make most of them, and different speeds would miss them. Normally, I did my damnedest to cruise through the lights. This time, I decided to drive slower and miss them. Anything to give me more time to devise a way out of this situation.

"What you mean we getting played? And where the hell you driving to?"

"You haven't told me where we're going yet," I said.

"Just picking up Franklin." We missed the light at Saratoga Street. "Might as well take a major road."

"Whatever," he muttered. "What's this shit about being played?"

"Those two kids who got killed before their mothers weren't in the gangs."

"Bullshit," my gun-toting passenger said.

"Did you know either of them?" I said.

"No. But I don't know every brother in this gang. Shit, probably a lotta 'em I ain't met."

"Maybe. But *no one* knew these kids. Not in the gangs and not in the police. They were good students at Morgan State. How many of those you have in the Bucs?"

"You saying we all stupid?"

"Just saying being a banger means you probably don't have the time to do well at college." We missed the light at Mulberry, too. So far, my strategy was working. Now I just had to figure out step two of my master plan.

"Don't mean they wasn't in the gang," he said.

"You're right. They weren't." He missed my jab at his double negative, so I added, "Someone wants you to think they were."

"Why?"

"So you'll shoot each other. The easiest way to get rid of Bucs and Pirates is to have you do it yourselves."

"My uncle Calvin says you just trying to stir up shit, man."

There was the connection. Calvin must have doubted my story at the support group. I wondered if he sent the two chuckleheads who threatened me, too. "Actually, I'm trying to stop the shit from being stirred. The police are finally starting to believe me."

He paused, obviously in thought. I allowed myself a flicker of hope. Then he said, "Just drive."

I shook my head. For a minute, I thought I got through to him for whatever good it might do. "Where are we going?" I said.

"You gonna meet the man."

I presumed he meant the Bucs' leader. "What's he want with me?"

"He wanna know everything you know. Then he wanna cut you. A lot. Probably cut you while he asking you questions."

"Sounds like a charmer." We missed our third straight light. Maybe I'd get lucky and all the assholes we were going to see would be arrested or dead by the time we arrived. "What do they call you?"

"Horse," he said.

"Why?"

"'Cause I'm hung like one." He puffed his chest out when he explained.

"I won't ask you to prove it," I said. I wondered how many times his long face got him compared to a horse as a child.

Horse chortled. What a silver-tongued devil I was: I could charm the pants off comely young women and get gang members to laugh when they pointed guns at me. The words would go nicely on my tombstone, which looked more and more like a looming part of my future. There was no way I could let Horse take me to meet the man. Even if he didn't cut me to ribbons, I knew I wouldn't walk out of the situation alive.

"How much farther is it?" I said as we waited for the light at Paca Street.

"Couple miles," Horse said.

A couple miles. Presuming we kept missing most of the lights—and Horse hadn't said anything about our progress yet—it gave me maybe five or six minutes to devise a way to survive this. Horse kept the gun trained on me, even though he didn't watch me all the time. Still, wrestling it away from him in a confined space, all while trying to keep a thirty-year-old Mustang on the road, struck me as a poor plan. I could try it at a red light, but I noticed he watched me more when we were stopped. Making a move on the road was risky, but I didn't see a better option.

I needed a window of opportunity, but simply because Horse didn't keep an eye on me a hundred percent of the time didn't make him inattentive. As we waited for the light at Carey Street, I put my hands in my lap. Horse noticed. I wanted him to. I did the same thing at the next light, too. If he got used to seeing it, then maybe he would take for granted I was doing it and not pay such close attention.

"You praying?" he said.

"What if I am?" I said.

"Ain't gonna help you none. The man still gonna find out what you know, and he still gonna cut you up."

"Jesus is my shield," I said as seriously as I could.

He snorted. "Shit, man. My momma believe all that shit. Jesus ain't never do nothing for us, y'know? I got a lot farther believing in the Bucs than in Jesus."

We'd hit another red signal in the meantime. Now we sat at Monroe Street. We came up on it when it was still yellow. I fought the urge to mash the gas, and instead hit the brake and waited. Monroe was a pretty major road. I saw a few cars and a couple trucks go by.

Trucks. An idea took shape.

Monroe Street ran one way southbound from our right to left. A break in traffic happened, meaning the light could change soon. I still needed a way out of this situation before meeting the man. A tractor, sans trailer, sped down Monroe. I looked at Horse. He watched the traffic. The tractor drew closer.

I moved my right hand off my lap and shoved the gun away from me. "What the fuck, man?" Horse said. He pushed against me, but I didn't give. He squeezed the trigger. My ears rang and felt like they would burst as the bullet shattered the windshield. The tractor was close now. If the driver heard the gunshot, he didn't show it. I waited until he was almost into the intersection, then I let the clutch out and stomped on the gas. If I went to the Bucs' base, I was dead. If this collision killed me, at least I chose my own death.

The truck driver realized what was about to happen. I heard his horn. Horse yelled beside me. He kept a strong grip on the gun. The truck driver's eyes widened. The cab cleared as the Mustang plowed into the rear of the tractor.

Metal twisted. Glass shattered. The tractor slid. The rear of the Ford came off the asphalt. Without the benefit of an airbag, my head crashed into the steering wheel. Horse, with no airbag or seatbelt, went out through the windshield, opening a much larger hole than the bullet did.

The Mustang crashed back to the road. My head

slammed into the headrest. Everything spun, then stars swam in front of my eyes before the lights went out.

CHAPTER 11

AMMONIA. MY BRAIN PROCESSED THE STRONG smell. There was no other awareness, just its scent flooding my nostrils. Air rushed into my nose, my eyes opened, and only then did I become aware of anything else. Horse's Mustang sat on its tires, but if I hadn't known what kind of car it was, I wouldn't have recognized its twisted and battered shell. I lay on the ground, looking up at a slender male EMT. His name tag was blurry, and I had trouble focusing on it, but it looked like it said "Stevenson."

Bits of broken glass lay all around me on the asphalt. I raised my head slowly. Waves of dizziness washed over me. I took a deep breath. Dents and scratches marred the back part of the tractor. I saw a fiftyish man with a bloody face, forearm tattoos, and a tattered baseball cap talking to a police officer. On some level, I remembered what I did: I deliberately gunned the pony car into the intersection and into the rear of a speeding tractor. The possibility of dying in the collision struck me as preferable to the slow, painful, and certain death awaiting me if Horse took me to meet the Bucs' higher-ups.

Horse . . . he exited stage front in the wreck. Stevenson's mouth moved, but I couldn't make out what he said. I eased my head back down and squinted up at him. "What?" I said.

"You shouldn't pick your head up," he said. "You might have a spinal injury, and movement would only make it worse."

I wiggled my fingers and toes. "I don't have a spinal injury." From somewhere behind me, I heard a brief argument. "How's the other guy?"

"The truck driver is shaken up, but he's not injured. Airbag deployed. He'll be fine."

"I meant the other guy in the car."

Stevenson frowned. "It doesn't look good. He went out the windshield, hit the tractor, then hit the street."

I shouldn't have felt bad, but I did. Then I heard a familiar voice.

"C.T., are you all right?" Rich said.

"Sure," I said. "Just resting here on the street."

"He has a concussion," Stevenson said. "Some cuts and bruises, maybe an internal injury or two. He should go to the hospital."

"Rubbish," I said, "there's a case to wrap up."

"Tell me what happened," said Rich. I told him. "Jesus Christ."

"I couldn't let him take me to the Buc base," I said.

"You couldn't have just run into a telephone pole?"

"I needed something to take him out of the equation." I shrugged. "When I saw the tractor speeding down the road, it seemed like the better option."

"You got lucky."

"Maybe. I need to tell you something, though." I raised my head again. No dizziness. It was progress. I sat up part of the way, propping myself up on my elbows, leading to an instant pain between my eyes.

"I really think you should just lie there," Stevenson said.

"No rest for the wicked," I said.

The headache lingered. I figured it would remain for a while at varying degrees of tolerability. Stevenson was right; I should have stayed on the asphalt. Despite the pain, I sat up. I nearly collapsed back to the street, but I fought the dizziness.

"Go to the hospital," Rich said.

"Later," I said. "Help me up." I stuck out my hand. Rich rolled his eyes and shook his head, but he grabbed my hand pulled me slowly upward. I went to my knees first, then to one knee before standing bent at the waist. Rich let go of my hand. My head swam, and noises sounded distorted and far away. Nausea tugged at my stomach. I put my hands on my knees and slowly straightened. I wish I could say it felt good, but it didn't. I felt miserable, like I would sink back to the street at any second. Rich looked at me with narrowed eyes. He held his hands ready to grab me. I took a few deep breaths, and the sickness lessened.

"Calvin," I said. "Calvin is the key." My brain became foggy. Why did I call him the key? The key to what?

"We can talk more after we get you to the hospital," Rich said.

"They could be ramping up. You've seen the shootings. No time for lying down on the job." I wanted to tell him something else—the name Reedy floated somewhere in the growing haze—but I couldn't retrieve it.

"Let us worry about it. You get some rest. King and I can talk to you later."

"It's important," I insisted. My mouth kept moving, but I couldn't figure out anything I said. I experienced the sensation of falling forward. Something stopped me. I looked around. Rich held me up. Somewhere in the distance, I heard him shout for the paramedics.

* * *

MY BRAIN CAME BACK to the land of the conscious before my body did. I knew I was lying down. It constituted the whole of my knowledge at this moment. I felt like I slept off a bender in college—foggy, disconnected, and with a headache. My mouth and throat were as dry as a skeleton baking in the desert. Voices coalesced into ones I recognized. My parents were in the room. A few seconds later, I found the self-awareness to open my eyes.

"Robert, he's awake," my mother said.

"I see that. Son, how are you?"

I looked around. I lay in a hospital bed. An IV ran into my arm, and electrodes for a heart monitor were attached to my chest. I didn't have any other tubes or gizmos connected to me. A small flatscreen TV mounted on the wall across the room displayed a commercial on mute. The bedside table had a cup of water atop it. "Thirsty," I said.

My mother handed me the cup of water. I drained it in one gulp. The dryness in my throat passed, and I let out a deep breath. My head still hurt, and I felt as if a layer of gauze stretched over everything. "Coningsby, the doctor says you have a concussion," she said.

"I'm sure I do," I said.

"What happened?"

I told her the story of Horse making me drive at gunpoint, where he wanted to take me, and the horrible things likely to happen there. It took me a few minutes to tell the story because I stopped and restarted a few times. Things got clearer as I went through it. My mother frowned when I finished. "That's terrible . . . having to make a choice like that," she said.

I shrugged. "It's a terrible world sometimes. Any news on the kid who carjacked me?"

"No," my father said. "I haven't asked. I don't really care what happens to him."

"Robert!" My mother's chiding tone hadn't changed since I first heard it as a toddler.

"Just being honest."

My father refilled my cup, and I drank more water. "You guys my first visitors?" I said.

"No," my mother said. "Richard was here a little while ago. I think you talked to him for a few minutes."

"I did?" I searched my memory for any recollection of this conversation and came up empty. Everything since I plowed the Mustang into the tractor was shrouded in fog.

"Yes, dear. He left in quite a hurry."

"I guess I told him something useful, then." My head throbbed, and everything got weird and distant again. "I think I'm going back to sleep."

My father said something, but his voice grew

distorted as if he were talking from underwater. Then I didn't hear him at all.

* * *

It felt like coming out of a deep sleep: My brain knew I was awake, but my body lodged its disagreement. My limbs felt like they were made of lead. Nary a noise came from the room. As the fog slowly lifted, I opened my eyes. My parents were gone, replaced by Rich and Captain Leon Sharpe. I looked at the bedside table; nurses refilled my water pitcher and cup. I grabbed the table, wheeled it closer, and drained the cup again. "How long have I been out?" I said.

"Almost a day," Rich said.

"Holy shit." Almost a day! How much did I miss lying in this hospital bed? "Did I tell you anything you could use?"

"Yeah, you managed to get it out before you went under again."

"And?" I said when Rich offered nothing else.

"And I put an emergency task force together," Sharpe said. "We got some people from the county and state. By and large, the members of the Pirates and Bucs are sitting in jail cells right now. Three of them died before we could round them up." He frowned. "We got them before the worst of it really started."

"What about Calvin and Reid?"

"No sign of them yet," Rich said.

The slippery bastards got away. "You came here just to deliver this cheery news?"

"And to see how you're doing."

"I'm as well as I can be," I said. "Which you could have learned by yourself."

"You want to know why I'm here," Sharpe said.

"I doubt police captains make many hospital room visits, even for handsome PIs who solve cases for them."

"You caused an accident."

"I prefer to think of it as avoiding torture and death," I said.

"The driver of the truck is probably going to sue you."

"I have insurance." I shook my head. It didn't hurt. Score one for progress. "He would have done the same thing in my spot." I looked at Sharpe for a second. "You would have, too, Leon."

"Probably," he said. "The kid in the car with you is alive. It was dicey for a while, but they think he's going to make it."

On some level, I felt glad to hear this news, but I kept it to myself.

Sharpe took an envelope from under his jacket and tossed it on the table. "Photos from the scene," he said. "My boss wanted me to come down here and chew your ass. I'm not going to. You made the same decision I would have made and he would have made. But he insisted I bring pictures so you could see 'the results of the fool's handiwork,' as he put it."

I poured some more water. The BPD commissioner could complicate my life if he wanted to. "Is he going to recommend my license be suspended?"

"No," said Sharpe. "I think he was just pissed that a PI managed to learn more about this case than his own cops."

"He'll get over it." I picked up the envelope and

opened it. The first picture told the story. Horse lay on the gurney after being extracted from the wreckage of the scene. From the pictures, I figured more of Horse's blood had spilled on the street than remained in his body. I couldn't believe he survived. Cuts from broken glass dotted his face, neck, and torso. The red turned his blue bandanna into a morose shade of purple.

I started to flip to the next photo, then stopped. Blood on the bandanna. It took me a moment to fight through the fog, but I remembered the photos I saw of the Dante Johnson and Andre Carter crime scenes. "Leon, I can prove those first two victims weren't gangbangers," I said.

"That would be nice, but I'm not sure it matters now."

"It matters to their families." I pulled the electrodes off my chest. Immediately, the heart monitor let out a cacophony of beeps and boops. "Rich and I will get Doctor Reid and Calvin. Maybe those two assholes in jail will matter to you." I looked down at the IV in my arm. It wasn't something I could just yank out. Three nurses sprinted into the room as I sat up. "What's going on?" the first one, a pretty Asian girl, said.

"Get this damn thing out of my arm," I said. "I'm going home."

"Sir, you were in a car accident. You have a concussion."

"There's a form I can sign to check out against medical advice, right?"

"C.T., we don't need to do this now," Rich said.

"Yes, we do. So . . . the form?"

"Uh . . . yes," she said, "you can check out against medical advice. I'll have to get the on-duty doctor."

"Good. Have him bring the paperwork for me to sign. But first, please take this goddamn thing out of my arm."

She did. The doctor came in a few minutes later and asked me to reconsider. He said I needed to stay for further observation. I pointed out what "against medical advice" meant and signed the form. Rich protested a couple times, but I think he knew the futility of it; Sharpe didn't even bother. After I collected my clothes, Rich drove me home.

We still needed to round up the instigators.

Rich parked at my curb and followed me to my door. Gloria texted as I walked in. She was concerned after not hearing from me for over a day. I smiled at her fretting over me. It was never part of the plan when we began our relationship. Now I wondered where it was headed. I would have to deal with it (and her) later, however. I fired off a quick reply telling her I was OK and busy wrapping up the gang mess.

"Here," Rich said, handing me my .45. "Uniforms found it on Horse. I knew it was yours. Not many HK45s out there."

I liked my Hechler and Koch. It was a little more accurate than the average .45, which made up for me being a good but not great shot. Plus, anyone who took a bullet from it dropped on the spot. I flashed back to helping Rich on an off-the-books case in western Maryland. I shot a goon three times in the chest before he could kill Rich. If I could have gone my whole career without putting the gun's stopping power to the test, I would have done so. Life doesn't always cooperate with our plans, however. If Calvin drew down on me, I'd be ready for him.

"What did you mean about proving those first two kids weren't gangbangers?" Rich said.

"Horse's bandanna," I said, "was soaked with blood."

"Sure."

"The first two kids' weren't. For all the blood they shed, their bandannas were pretty dry. Like someone put it on their heads after the fact."

"Huh." Rich nodded. If I didn't know him better, I might have said he was impressed.

"Tell me where you've looked for Reid and Calvin," I said.

"Everywhere we could think of." Rich ran a hand through his short hair. "Both their houses, where they work, known associates. . . ."

"And you came up empty?"

"Yeah. They're in the wind."

"What about ways out of town?" I asked.

"We're covering those," said Rich. "They can't get on a plane, train, or bus without us knowing about it."

I shrugged. "They can get an Uber, though, and you'll never know."

"You're a wet blanket."

"Wow," I said.

"What?"

"I don't think anyone has been called a wet blanket in about twenty years."

"It's not so old a term," Rich protested.

"Whatever you say, daddy-o."

He rolled his eyes. "You can't be concussed too badly. Your annoying sense of humor is the same as ever."

I grinned and after a moment, so did Rich. "What about the support group?" I said.

"What support group?"

"Sounds like you haven't checked it, then. Reid and Calvin run a session to aid people affected by gang violence. It might be the one good thing they do."

"And you know where these people meet?" Rich said. I nodded. "Let me guess—you crashed one of their meetings." I inclined my head again; Rich moved his on the opposite axis. "You're unbelievable sometimes. People are there because they need help."

"Now who's a wet blanket?" I said. Rich glared at me. "I didn't prevent anyone from getting help. I simply scoped it out and snagged a member roster."

Rich took a deep breath. He probably felt the roster was the bridge too far. Without it, I wouldn't have learned who Calvin was so quickly. While my natural brilliance may have led me there at some point, more casualties could have happened in the interim. "Could you tell me where they meet?"

"Yes," I said.

He waited. "Well? Where?"

"I'll be glad to show you en route." I put my hand up when Rich voiced an objection. "I'm coming along. This is my case, too."

"Fine," Rich said after stewing a few seconds. "I'm calling in Paul King, too."

"The more, the merrier," I said.

* * *

Outside the church or store or whatever the hell it had been, Rich and King strapped on Kevlar. King tossed me a vest, and I did the same. "I'm touched," I said.

"Rich would cry if you got shot," he said.

"You know me," Rich said. "I'd weep for days."

While I put the bullet-resistant armor on, I described the general layout of the place for the rest of the raiding party. Doctor Reid and Calvin were likely to be downstairs, as the upper floor didn't offer much in the way of furnishings or cover. Rich and King checked their weapons. This struck me as an excellent idea, so I followed suit. "Let's go," Rich said.

The outside door was secured with the shabby kind of lock an old store should have, and I got us inside in about a minute. We didn't hear any alarms. Rich and King both drew their guns. Never one to be left out, I unholstered mine, too. They both stalked around the first floor with their heavy-duty flashlights. My LED model looked puny by comparison.

"Clear," Rich said in a quiet voice a moment later.

"They must be downstairs," King said. "You guessed right."

"Don't sound so surprised," I said. We moved to the stairs.

"I'll cover you," Rich said as we stood at the top. King went first, his pistol and flashlight leading the way. I descended next. Toward the bottom of the staircase, my head started to hurt. When I cleared the final step, balance became an issue. Nausea clawed at my insides. I slumped into the wall, grateful for the support. "You sure you're OK?" King whispered.

I nodded. He didn't look convinced. I couldn't blame

him—I didn't feel convinced, either. "I just need a minute," I said.

"What's going on?" Rich said as he joined us. He looked at me and frowned. "You really shouldn't be here."

"Bullshit," I said. "I'm proving my championship mettle by playing hurt."

"Let us take the lead," King said. "You got us here." He jerked his head toward the door a couple feet away. "Pick this lock and call it a night."

I pushed off the wall, took a couple uncertain steps, and tried the knob. Locked. I put my gun away, took out my tools, and crouched. Even such a simple action sent my equilibrium askew again. I used a hand to steady myself and took a couple deep breaths until the waves of sickness passed.

"Work from the side as much as you can," King whispered. "If they hear you messing with the lock, they might shoot."

"Worst pep talk ever," I said.

"I don't do pep talks."

"Good thing," I said as I knelt to the side of the door. Working from an angle would slow me, but if it lowered my chances of getting shot, I could take the hit to my pride a sluggish lock-picking time would cause. Rich and King stood behind me, out of the way of any gunfire.

A couple minutes later, I popped the bolt. King materialized on the other side of me as if he had been transported those few feet. I stood. Rich and King both nodded, and Rich opened the door. They both pointed their guns through the opening. The only things to greet us were silence and darkness.

I stood, walked in behind them, and stuck to the wall on the right. At least I didn't feel like I needed it to keep me vertical at the moment. King kept to the left. Rich took the middle of the room.

"Rich, light," King whispered.

"Go ahead," Rich said.

King flipped a switch, and fluorescent brightness flooded the room. "They have to know we're here already," he said.

Quiet voices came from the office, but I couldn't make out anything being said. Rich and King both stared in its direction. We stood about where the semicircle of chairs was setup for the support group. The office door clicked and someone dragged it open about a foot. Two small hands appeared in the doorway. "Don't shoot," Doctor Reid said.

"Come out with your hands up," King said as he moved closer to the door. He kept his gun on Reid the whole time. So did Rich. I didn't like the fact of Reid showing after a conversation. Where was Calvin, and what did he have planned?

"I'm not resisting," Reid said. He stepped out from the office, pulling the door shut behind himself.

King dragged him out into the center of the area. "Maurice Reid, you are under arrest," he said, replacing his pistol with a pair of handcuffs. He Mirandized Reid as Rich and I looked on.

"I don't like this," I whispered. "Where's Calvin? We know he's a shooter."

"You said the office has a second door, right?" Rich said.

"Yeah, around the corner."

"Keep an eye on it, then." We both moved in. Reid was cuffed and on his knees. King finished reading him his rights. Footsteps came from around the corner.

"You fuckers ain't takin' me alive!" Calvin said.

"Calvin, don't do this," Reid implored. "It's over. We lost. There's no need for anyone to get shot."

"I ain't going back to jail," Calvin hollered from the hidden hallway. King ushered Reid toward the entrance door.

"Calvin Terrell, come out with your hands up," Rich said.

"Fuck you," Calvin said. He came around the corner with a large revolver in his hand. He swung it toward Rich and me. We both fired. Bullets rocked Calvin. His revolver pointed toward the floor. Rich and I watched him, guns still at the ready. Calvin looked at us, then at the gun he held by his side, then pitched forward.

"Calvin!" Reid yelled from outside the main door.

* * *

Rich, King, and I all gave our statements. King drew the short straw and went downtown to fill out more paperwork. Rich and I drove back to my house. "We couldn't do anything else but shoot," Rich said after a few minutes of glorious silence.

I nodded. "I know." I didn't say anything else. Knowing I was forced to shoot Calvin and dealing with it were two different things. He was the second person circumstances impelled me to fire upon. When I got into this job, I envisioned sitting behind my desk and hacking my way to whatever solution the case required. I never thought I would need to shoot anyone.

"How do you feel?"

"Tired," I said. "I may also admit to having some lingering concussion symptoms."

"I mean about the shooting," Rich said.

I thought about it for a moment. "It was easier this time." Again, I lapsed into silence.

"It bothers you."

"Shouldn't it?"

"Probably," Rich said. "You did what had to be done. It was him or us. I'm sure it'll take a few days to sort it all out."

"Did it take you a few days?" I said.

Now Rich fell silent. After a moment, he said, "For me, it was a week into my first tour in Afghanistan. Same thing—it was him or me. I knew I was right. It took me a couple days to process it and come out the other side. I still remember every detail today, though, even down to the blood." He paused. "Especially the blood."

"Did it get easier?"

"You mean as I killed more people?" I bobbed my head. "Yeah, it does. It might sound messed up, but as long as the shootings are legit, you're just coming to terms with everything faster. You're adapting. It's normal."

"I don't know if it's normal," I said, "but I understand. And I guess I'm going to have to deal with it."

"I've been through it. You can always talk to me if you need to."

"Thanks," I said.

We made the rest of the drive in silence. Nothing else needed to be said.

* * *

THE NEXT DAY, I went through the usual conversation with my mother after wrapping up a case. She was proud of what I did but horrified as always about man's inhumanity to man. They would pay me the usual rate for a job well done. I was technically a contract employee of my parents' foundation, and the money for solving cases constituted a salary.

Later, I talked to the press. Reid and Calvin staging the initial shootings to gin up the gangs made for quite a story. I emailed my proof Dante Johnson and Andre Carter weren't gang members to local reporter Jessica Webber. She would have a few details no one else would. Jessica chronicled my first case, though I hadn't seen her much since it ended.

I also talked to Erma Johnson. It was the longest and most worthwhile conversation of the day. Several times, she said, "I told you my grandson wasn't in no gang."

I said, "Yes, ma'am" every time.

THE END

Hi! Thanks for reading this novella. I hope you enjoyed reading it as much as I did writing it.

Here are the other books in my catalog:

The C.T. Ferguson Crime Novels:

1. The Reluctant Detective
2. The Unknown Devil
3. The Workers of Iniquity
4. Already Guilty
5. Daughters and Sons
6. A March from Innocence
7. Inside Cut
8. The Next Girl
9. In the Blood
10. Right as Rain
11. Dead Cat Bounce (December 2021)

The C.T. Ferguson Crime Novellas:

1. The Confessional (book 1.5 in overall series continuity)
2. Land of the Brave (2.5)
3. Red City Blues (3.5)
4. Blood on Canvas (8.5)

The John Tyler Action Thrillers

1. The Mechanic
2. White Lines
3. Lost Highway
4. Four on the Floor (Spring 2022)

While these are the suggested reading sequences, each novel is a standalone mystery or thriller, and the books can be enjoyed in whatever order you happen upon them.

Do you like free books? You can get the prequel novella to the C.T. Ferguson mystery series for free. *Hong Kong Dangerous* is unavailable for sale and is exclusive to my readers. Visit https://www.subscribepage.com/hkd2020 to get your book!

Connect with me:

For the many ways of finding and reaching me online, please visit https://tomfowlerwrites.com/contact. I'm always happy to talk to readers.

This is a work of fiction. Characters and places are either fictitious or used in a fictitious manner.

"Self-publishing" is something of a misnomer. This book would not have been possible without the contributions of many people.

- The great cover design team at 100 Covers.
- My editor extraordinaire, Chase Nottingham.
- My wonderful advance reader team, the Fell Street Irregulars.